WOMAN CHIEF

Taken as a captive by the Crow Indians, she began her life in this strange tribe as "Slave Girl." She would later be revered as *Woman Chief*.

In a taboo-ridden world, where men were warriors and women were laborers, Slave Girl possessed skills and confidence unheard-of among her sex. She tamed the wild stallion that no one could ride, joined the buffalo hunt uninvited, and took the scalp of a notorious enemy.

She was known to white traders and explorers of her time as the legendary "Absaroka Amazon."

WOMAN CHIEF

Benjamin Capps

GUNSMOKE

This hardback edition 2002
by Chivers Press
by arrangement with
Golden West Literary Agency

ISBN 0 7540 8179 6

British Library Cataloguing in Publication Data available.

Printed and bound in Great Britain by
BOOKCRAFT, Midsomer Norton, Somerset

To
Holly Lynn Capps,
who is just the same age as this book

NOTE

The native peoples of North America differed greatly from one another in their customs and manners, their means of livelihood, their regulation of the sexes, their values, laws, religions. However, the people of the Plains, the horse Indians, all had one belief in common: it was a man's world. The warriors killed the meat, raided the enemy, defended the band, made the decisions. Females were good for sex and caring for babies and cooking and gathering wood and water, a hundred simple tasks.

Strangely, among the Crow, or Absarokas, in that land along the Yellowstone River, grew up a girl who was the great exception. They called her Woman Chief. She became a legend among white traders and explorers as the "Absaroka Amazon." One of the most amazing Americans of her day, she defied the limitations placed upon her sex and made the fierce warriors of the northern plains respect her.

Woman Chief's story is handed down to us by Edwin Thompson Denig, for twenty-three years a trader for the American Fur Company on the upper Missouri, and the story is confirmed by explorer Rudolph Kurz and others. This novel follows the truthful outline of Woman Chief's life, as it is known. The present writer has profited much from the works of later scholars such as Frank Linderman and John Ewers.

The reader should be aware that the present writer admires and respects the Sioux, the Cheyenne, the Blackfeet, and their allies. Where any insult against these peoples appears in this novel, it is a legitimate reflection of Crow, or Absaroka, attitudes of a century and a half ago.

B. Capps, Grand Prairie, Texas

1. The Capture

The raiding party of Crow Indians had spied on the enemy village for two days, sending their wolves to scout around it in all directions to make certain that no other enemies camped in the vicinity. Crow leader Elk Head lay on his belly on a rise a mile from the village on the second evening and plotted with his senior warriors.

"Post sentinels tonight and sleep," he said. "Rise before first light. Wait till they bring out the choice horses toward the flood plain over there. The first party cuts them off. One gun goes with the first party. When you are between the horses and the village, fire it off. Head the horses straight west for the raid camp. You should get there by sundown tomorrow. Remember, if you get all the horses, especially the good ones, they can't come after us."

The warrior beside him asked, "Who gets first choice on the horses? Will you go with the horse party?"

"I'll go with the party that hits the village. The horses and all booty will be divided in a way that is fair."

The warrior grunted his assent.

"Now, the village party," Elk Head continued.

"We cross the creek at first light. Right where the tallest cottonwood trees are. When we hear the gun fire off, we attack and yell. The other three guns go with us. Fire as fast as you can load. I don't care if you hit anything. Fire! Fire! Make them think we are many guns.

"Give them plenty of room to run downstream. Yell and fire! Go ahead with bows and clubs and knives. Take saddles, powder, blankets, cooking pots, whatever gear you see. Try to get some fresh meat; we don't have time to hunt. I want two or three scalps to dance under, men if possible. Load up your mounts with loot and come out. Do not take any captives."

A warrior behind a clump of sage rose to a squatting position. "Wait! We have an agreement, Elk Head!"

"Get down," the leader said. "You are sitting against the sky. Where did you learn the skills of raiding?"

"You know me good and well."

"I know you, Antelope Man. Get down. Captives are nothing but trouble. I want two or three scalps and the horses and the best camp gear. I don't want to get any of us killed."

"I'm going to catch a ten-year-old boy. I told you about it and you agreed."

"Look, Antelope Man, these are Hairy Noses, Big Bellies. They are not fit for slaves, much less to take the place of a dead son."

"I'll make a good Crow out of him."

Someone else said, "Why don't you capture a baby, Antelope Man. Then you can rear him right."

"The women protect them too well. I would

have to kill the mother."

"Are you against killing a Hairy Nose woman?"

"I would kill one. But not the mother of my boy."

Still another man said, "What's the matter, Antelope Man? Are you too old to make a woman pregnant yourself?"

They laughed, but Elk Head said, "All right, that's enough. Does everyone know the plan? One captive. One boy for Antelope Man. That's all. Let's get some sleep. It's a big day tomorrow."

They took a last look at the enemy village, which clustered in a bend of the creek. It was made up of some twenty skin-covered tepees. Here and there the figure of a man, woman, or child could be seen passing among the lodges. Thin smoke of cook fires wafted along the tops of the tepees and into the trees. The Crow raiders fixed the lay of the land in their minds and one by one slid backward down the high ground of their observation point.

They wore no bright metal ornaments or feathers, but were stripped for stealthy war. Two of them even had mud from the creek plastered in their hair and smeared on face, neck, shoulders, and chest. They made no sound as they crept away in the twilight.

The Crow, or Absarokas, considered themselves the greatest horse thieves of all time. They made an art of it. Their land lay south of Elk River, which the white traders called the Yellowstone, and they were pressed by many enemies. Besides the Atsinas, which they contemptuously called Hairy Noses or Big Bellies, there were the mighty Dakotas and the Blackfoot tribes. The Crows determined to retreat no farther from their foes, to give back raid for raid, to prove their right to their bountiful hunting lands. If they could not meet their better armed and more numerous enemies in open battle, they would meet them by stealth. It seemed amazing to them how often their tactics of surprise worked.

The following morning in the dim dawn, Elk Head took the larger band of his raiding force through the timber to a creek ford beaten out by the crossing of buffalo. He had guessed the wind right. It blew toward them. They led their horses through the knee-deep water, making only a soft swishing sound. They waited, the twenty-one warriors, hidden by a clump of plum bushes, each standing ready to clamp his hand over the nose of his horse to smother any snort or snicker.

The innocent village came awake slowly with the murmur of sleepy voices high and low, sometimes laughter. The smell of twigs catching fire and burning rose in the air, later the smell of broiling meat. Some women were headed toward the creek to dip water. When the boys began to drive out the choice horses, which had been tied in camp, their voices could be heard calling to one another, but the horses' hoofs made only a soft thudding in the valley soil.

The sun had risen to the treetops when the BOOM! of a gun sounded on the prairie. Elk Head hissed "Now!" They mounted, raced around the edge of the thicket, and began yelling war cries. Those three with guns fired them wildly; puffs of dirty smoke burst from the muzzles.

Screams sounded from the village, and shocked questioning cries. The largest, most aggressive dog came toward the invaders, barking furiously. A

Crow bowman hit him in one hind leg, and he turned yelping through the village. He led the exodus downstream.

The Atsinas might have defended better, but they were not ready. As the shouting Crows came into the edge of the tepees, the villagers seemed to be presented with two choices; run or die. Many of them ran. Here and there both men and women took a short stand with bow or club to allow time for children or old people to escape. A man ran back to rescue his painted shield from a tripod by his lodge and went down with an arrow through his back, the bloody point protruding in front. A woman emerged from her tepee with enough blankets and rawhide boxes to load a horse; she was clubbed down, not so much for her scalp as for her possessions. Confusion reigned for some minutes, with much shouting and screaming. The three guns along with two or three that answered them, blasted loudly in the valley air and raised a raw and acrid pall of smoke. At one edge of the ravaged village the raiders could see Antelope Man frantically trying to shake a slender figure from the sloping branch of a cottonwood tree; the man finally found an ax and chopped the branch down.

Elk Head charged and wheeled his horse on the village paths, yelling instructions. The horse paused awkwardly to defecate a knobby pile where the main path forked to lead to the water hole in the creek, and the raiders pointed and cheered. They had taken the camp. Whatever they could pack out was theirs. In short order they piled their mounts with booty and led them west.

They strung out over the rolling prairie in clumps of two or three or four. They were exultant,

shouting to one another, laughing. As they came
over a swell of high ground, they could see ahead
two miles the dust and movement of the enemy
horse herd their comrades had taken.

Of those who had hit the village only one rode—
Antelope Man. Part of the time he rode. Sometimes he tried to walk alongside his horse and balance his burden across it. He was trying to trans-
port a buffalo robe that was rolled around something that seemed alive.

A warrior yelled at him, "Did you have good
luck, Antelope Man?"

"I caught me a wildcat," he called back. The uncertainty in his voice caused them to look at him.
The side of his face from forehead to chin had
bloody marks down it, as if it had been ripped by
sharp claws.

"Hey!" someone said. "You must have got the
toughest Hairy Nose boy they had!"

"The bravest anyway," Antelope Man laughed.
"I hope he calms down so I can lead him on a rope.
I can't carry him this way."

At that time they saw two horsemen racing toward them from the rear; it was the wolves who
had followed the enemy a short distance. The
Crows, some dozen of them, gathered and waited
to hear any news. The wolves said that there would
be no pursuit. Some of the Hairy Noses were
sneaking back to their village, but they had scarcely a half dozen sorry horses left.

Antelope Man clumsily eased his burden to the
ground. They gathered around. "Let us see your
great prize, Antelope Man." "Sure, let's see him;
you don't get a full horse share, you know." "I
want to see what tore up his face that way."

He unrolled the robe almost gently. He looked up at them and asked seriously, "Please don't scare him," then pushed the covering open.

The little creature sat up blinking its black eyes. It looked around at them all. It was a ten-year-old girl.

Antelope Man was a middle-aged warrior of fair reputation. Unfortunately he could not help showing his feelings. He was mortified.

They began to chuckle and jibe. "Hey, he caught a she wildcat!" "I thought you already had a lodge full of females!" "You got a little split-tail girl, Antelope Man!" It began to strike them as funnier and funnier. They slapped each other on the back and roared. They had felt tension since long before dawn and now, exultant over the success of the raid, they needed something to relax with. They seemed unable to stop laughing.

Antelope Man could not laugh. The girl frowned at the men as if she knew they were all foolish. She edged nearer to her captor. His chagrin was obviously deep. He might have killed the child if they had not laughed. He tried a time or two to answer them, to give some excuse, then awkwardly jerked the girl toward his horse. Taking a thin rope of rawhide, he tied it around her neck, folded the robe over his horse's back, mounted, and led his captive on west. His fellow raiders followed, still finding great humor in his error.

They moved without pause over the rolling plains. The girl had on good moccasins, as well as a deerskin dress and leggings. She had to pay careful attention walking through the sagebrush and bunch grass and prickly pear, not to stumble, lest she be dragged. In the middle of the afternoon, it became hot. The sun burned in their faces. She untied the knot at her neck and walked along holding onto the thin rope.

Antelope Man did not notice the change for a while; then he glanced back and shouted, "Did I say you could do that?"

He got down and began retying the rope. "Who do you think you are? You're a slave! And no good!"

He remounted and rode ahead grumbling. "You made a fool out of me. What are you doing climbing trees anyway?" With his hand gingerly touching the scratches on his face, he said, "You don't be good, I'll cut your throat."

Before sunset they came to their raid camp beside a pool of water in a clearing surrounded by sumac brush. They had selected it as a place to gather in the event that they ran into bad luck, and they had left three wolves with a few spare horses. The raiding band, totaling thirty-three men, had started out with forty horses and now had more than two hundred, besides some twenty pack loads of new property.

They appealed to Elk Head as to whether it was safe to build fires and he said, "Yes. We'll post wolves in every direction. I'm hungry. Let's cook some fresh fat meat. We'll divide the booty tonight and the horses tomorrow."

As darkness approached, four large fires blazed. Elk Head had appointed four special helpers, and these went about distributing the stolen goods into separate piles for the warriors. They broiled fresh buffalo and deer meat, cutting it off in hand-size pieces as it became done. There was much joking and laughter.

They still teased Antelope Man. He sat near a fire with eight or ten others, saying little. The captive girl squatted beside him, tearing with her teeth at a piece of hot meat. The talk drifted to the condition of the meat, buffalo and deer, enough to last them two or three days; it would surely spoil wrapped up tomorrow. They decided it must be cut in strips, hung on drying racks, and smoked through the night. They began to set up crude racks of small limbs.

Antelope Man put the girl to work cutting the meat into thin strips. A man said, "Hey, that Hairy Nose boy is doing woman's work!" Another said, "I'm going to look and see for sure if she's a girl or boy!"

"Leave her alone," Antelope Man said.

The teasing man grabbed for her and said, "Here, I want to see if you are a boy or girl!"

She jerked back, half dragging, half carrying a hindquarter of deer. Then he began to chase her around the two flint-hide halves on which the meat lay. Several laughed at his horseplay. He lunged and started to shout; he did not see that she had placed both hands on the shank of the deer leg and lifted it.

She swung and struck him solidly in the side of the face. He fell back. The laughter stopped.

The man grunted in anger and began to rise. The girl brandished the hindquarter with her slender arms. Her eyes flashed defiantly in the firelight.

Antelope Man drew his hunting knife and stepped in front of the man. "I said leave her alone!"

"I'm going to break her neck!"

"You are going to leave her alone!"

"I think you are crazy, Antelope Man. You

draw your knife on me when I was only playing. Over a worthless Hairy Nose slave."

"Go play somewhere else."

"Antelope Man, you are crazy. I know what's the matter. You're too old to father a son and you're afraid you're getting too old to raid and steal one. So you're mad at everybody."

Antelope Man said, "If it's true, then it's my misfortune, not yours."

"Nobody will ever raid with you again. We have had a big success, and now we need a little fun. I'm moving to another fire, where there's no sore-foot bears."

His last remark raised a small chuckle, and he began to move his pile of property. The girl returned to cutting the meat into thin strips and putting them on the racks in the erratic smoke downwind of the fire.

About the time that many of them were lying down to sleep, the turn came for Antelope Man to serve as a watch, or wolf. Without a word, the girl followed him through the moonlight. He went down around the water hole and up a long slope to a high place, from which he could see many miles of the dimly lighted terrain. He sat down on a rock. She stood a while, then sat on the ground a little distance away. When he turned to look in one direction or another she turned to look the same way.

Faintly, from far distances around them, came the lonely howls of coyotes or wolves. Sometimes certain of the calls were answered by Antelope Man. He would stand and cup his hands at his mouth and make the high-pitched, drawn-out sound. A listener might have heard no difference at first and would have had to pay careful attention to understand that three of the wolves in the vast night were Absarokas.

The rest of the time he sat in silence, as did the girl. They thought their own thoughts. The Earth Mother has a stronger influence at night, though she sleeps. In her veins course the ever pulsings of the magic of life and being. For two quiet watchers, distractions do not catch the mind. Starlight and moonlight bathe gently the infinite contours of the Earth Mother's body, and she does not end at the horizon, but stretches on forever. In day, one must travel to know it, but at night the distance comes to one, and the wolves, even those too far away to hear, send back in thought the eternity of the Earth Mother.

She speaks her silent whispers the same in Absaroka or Atsina. To those who have ears inside their hearts, she speaks the same to a middle-aged warrior and to a ten-year-old girl child. The man would not admit that the girl must stay near him for her own protection, and she would not claim his protection, but merely take it.

On the second day of their journey toward home Antelope Man rode and trailed two ropes behind him, one pulling a pack horse, the other the captive girl. At the horse dividing, Elk Head had given him only one horse, a bony gray pack animal; the leader had exercised diplomacy in portioning out the horses. Since Antelope Man had spent his attention during the attack in securing a captive, he got less in booty than the others.

Of property other than horses Antelope Man had received these items. One pack saddle. Four

flint-hide halves, which had to be soaked in water
before they could be folded. One beaver skin. One
copper kettle. Three butcher knives with wooden
handles. One hand mirror. Two robes, well tanned.
A package of one dozen unsharpened iron ar-
rowheads. Nineteen yards of red and green calico
cloth. One bag of salt (Elk Head's favorites had
gotten sugar and coffee).

They had traveled only a short distance this day
when the girl removed the rope from around her
neck and carried it in her hand. Soon he glanced
back, then shouted at her, "Did I say you could do
that?" But he did not stop. He said to himself as
much as to her, "What am I going to do with you?"

Before the sun had risen a quarter way in the
sky, she began leaning against the shoulder of the
gray pack horse with one arm over him. At a con-
venient spot on the trail she seized his mane and
scrambled up to perch astride his withers. She still
held the rope. Antelope Man looked around and
repeated several times, "What am I going to do
with you? What am I going to do with you?"

That night in camp she helped unpack and water
and hobble the horses as if she were a member of
the family. He tolerated her with disgust. After
they had eaten, she brought a piece of leafy vine to
show him as if it were important; she had found it
growing in the edge of camp. He frowned and
grunted and sat down on the ground with his back
against a tree.

From their pile of property she took the small
hand mirror. She came and knelt near him and
began chewing the leaves from the piece of vine
and spitting them on the mirror. "What are you
doing?" he demanded. "Did I say you could do
that?" She held up the vine to show him, then con-

tinued chewing the leaves carefully and spitting them on the mirror. When she had a pile half as big as her fist, she began stirring it with her finger, sometimes adding more saliva. Then she came toward him.

"Get away!" he said. "What do you think you're doing?"

She moved gently, holding out a dab of the green chewed mess on one finger.

"Get away! I'm going to beat you!"

She got the vine and showed it to him again.

"I don't care what you think you're doing, get away from me!"

She put some of the mixture on her cheek. He got up and moved away from her, sitting down by another tree. When she moved toward him again, he said, "You are going to get a beating."

She moved with the mirror in front of her and her finger outstretched, as slowly as if approaching an injured dog that might bite. He glared at her. She stepped slightly to one side, leaned out and gently put the crushed green leaves to his scratched face. He submitted in disgust. At first she doctored him with one finger, tentatively, then became as busy as a mother caring for a baby, patting the mixture all over the side of his face.

They stood guard again that night, two wolves alone on a hilltop.

The following day he put the rope about her neck as usual, but the party was no sooner under way than she removed it and mounted the bony gray pack horse. He kept looking back at her, but said nothing. The raiding party with their horse herd became strung out widely; they were now safely in Crow country.

Antelope Man pulled even farther apart from

the others and dismounted. He motioned her to get down. "I am setting you free," he said. "You don't understand, but listen carefully. Follow the tracks backward. You can find your way. Tracks, see, tracks."

He pointed at the tracks the horses had just made. He walked a few steps in the direction they had come, bending over, looking at the ground. "You. Tracks, see. You. You can go home. Go back that way."

She stared at him solemnly.

"Here, you can have some meat." He dug into the pack, brought out some chunky strings of black dry meat, and handed them to her.

"Now, you go. Understand? You. Go back. Free. Go back."

She stared at him.

"Now watch my signs, you stupid little girl. You. Go. Father, you. Mother, you. Understand? Go home to your mother and father. Follow the tracks and take the meat and go back to your mother and father."

The Atsina girl began to make signs. First, a baby against one's left breast—Mother. Then Me. Then tapping the chest with the fingers, Man, the forefinger up—Father. Then Me. My Mother and Father. Then the girl made an unusual sign, her fingers spread and curved as if for rain or hail, but not down, rather into her own face.

"What did they do? What happened to them?"

Mother, Me, she signed. Father, Me. Then the strange sign. She said something in the foreign language that the Atsina speak, then said, "Smaw Pok. Smaw Pok."

He said the dreaded English word they had

learned from white traders, "Smallpox?"

She nodded.

"Are they dead?"

She did not understand.

"Your mother and father. Did they die?" He made the signs. Mother and Father, Question. Dead?

She was not so adept at signs as he. She made the signs; Mother, Me. Father, Me. Sleeping. No good, throw it away.

He walked around a minute, gazing out over the boundless prairie. "I can't help it. You will have to go back. I can't keep you."

She went and got the extra rope from the pack and tied it around her neck and tried to hand the end of it to him.

He began to rail at her, "Don't you understand? You stupid little girl! I dreamed! I had a vision! I captured a boy. The spirit of my dead son was in him. He was mine alive again!

"Don't you understand? I would teach him to ride and hunt and he would become the greatest warrior in the Crow Nation. I dreamed he was not afraid of thunder! Our people would make up songs about him! They would sing his name!"

She had replaced the rope and the dry strings of meat in the pack. She stood listening, her face somewhat reflecting the anguish that appeared in his. She clenched her tiny fists when he clenched his.

"Don't you see? He would be a great warrior! He was not afraid of thunder! I dreamed it was true! No, you don't see. You don't see. How could you understand?"

He waited a minute in helpless frustration, looking around at the plains and at the straggling raid party going away. He mounted his horse and went after them. Immediately she swung onto the pack horse and followed, kicking her heels into the shoulders of the bony gray to make him keep up.

After some time Antelope Man started grumbling as he rode. "I don't deserve this. I'm an honorable man with coups, a proud man. I have my pride.

"Four women in my lodge. One skinny aunt. One mother-in-law who tries to boss things and custom does not allow me to speak to her. Two wives I've had so long I cannot send them back and get my purchase price back. Four women. And sometimes they sass me.

"Who will kill the meat for my lodge when I am old? Who will kill the skins so that we will be a wealthy family? Who will go to war and defend our honor?

"I don't deserve this. They won't bring the pipe to me to go on raids anymore. They will say I'm too old. Or too funny.

"I see what's happened. It's clear enough. Captured. I got captured myself. By a ten-year-old Big Belly female. One that climbs trees, like a squirrel or possum."

2. Slave Girl

At first in the home village of the Crow band the new captive was hardly noticed. Wolves went ahead to the camp to insure a proper reception. The raiders wanted to parade their captured horses and the two scalps and to receive the congratulations of everyone. However, Antelope Man turned out into the trees away from the others and approached his lodge so as to be unseen by his neighbors.

The members of his lodge were Broken Ice, his mother-in-law, Pea Finder, his aunt, and See Dead Bull and Birdy, his first and second wives. These lived together in one large tepee, ruled over by See Dead Bull, with much advice and aid from her mother, Broken Ice.

Only Pea Finder, a hump-shouldered old woman, was near when Antelope Man approached with his two horses and captive. The other women had gone toward the center of the village, where the camp crier yelled out the news and two of his assistants beat on flint-hide halves to attract attention. Pea Finder exclaimed, "Antelope Man! Antelope Man!" then scurried after the other family members.

Having seen that Antelope Man was not in the parade, the three hurried back immediately.

Within earshot of the returning master of the lodge, old Broken Ice said to her daughters, "Well, that husband of yours seems to think he's too good to ride with the others. Or is he ashamed to?"

Birdy went straightaway to Antelope Man where he had dismounted and hugged his arm. She began to ask if he was hungry or wanted anything.

Broken Ice said, "What has that husband of yours brought? Is he taking another wife at his age?"

"Tell that mother of yours," Antelope Man said, "that I don't need criticism right now. I'm worn out."

The captive girl had got down. She waited by the gray horse.

"She's too little and skinny for a slave," See Dead Bull said. "Why did you bring her?"

"That is my business," he said.

Broken Ice said, "It seems like your husband would know that we don't need another mouth to feed."

"Tell your mother this is my lodge and I kill the meat and I will feed as many as I please. I want all this hard talking stopped right now. Didn't I just come home safely from a dangerous raid? Didn't I bring a good gray horse and property and presents for the women of my lodge?"

They began to unload the packs from the gray horse and to exclaim over the stolen items. Everything was welcome, but all of it would belong to the family at large except the hand mirror and new calico. Pea Finger took the mirror. See Dead Bull took it away from her. Antelope Man intervened and gave it to Birdy. The four women unrolled the red and green bolts of cloth on the ground and discussed dividing it. Broken Ice and See Dead Bull decided that it should not be equally divided in fourths, for Pea Finder, being small, would get more blouses or dresses or capes or head shawls; therefore, they should keep the calico intact and portion it out to the four of them as the two of them deemed fair. As these discoveries and decisions proceeded, the captive Atsina girl stood back watching like a small animal looking out of the brush; if she knew whom the beautiful bright cloth had once belonged to and what the earlier plans had been for its use, she did not try to say, and the members of her new lodge did not guess that she had any thoughts or memories at all.

Now that he had demonstrated his prowess by showing the treasures he had brought to the women, Antelope Man took tentative control of the household. He asked what food they had on hand, then sent See Dead Bull, a good trader, to canvass the neighbors, taking the plundered beaver skin, or plew, to see what she might get for it in the way of coffee and sugar, with perhaps a quarter of fresh elk thrown in for boot.

He inquired about his horse herd of twenty animals and learned that they were doing well, though no one had seen them for two days. They undoubtedly grazed safely with others of the some five hundred Crow horses that were scattered over the miles of grass around the village. He took the horse he had been riding and the bony gray and hobbled them a short walk from camp.

The captive Atsina girl began that evening to try to discover how she might fit into the lodge of

Antelope Man. She watched them eat, standing back and waiting, and biding her time, until no one stood near the simmering kettle of meat and prairie turnips. She took a horn and filled it quickly and adroitly, getting chunks of meat to satisfy her hunger. She stood back then in the shadows, not to be interrupted while she kept from burning her hands and lips as she ate the rich stew.

When they went to bed, she watched carefully. If she would have liked to sleep near Antelope Man, it was impossible, for that spot was taken by Birdy. Finally, when all were settled, she lay down on the edge of a robe occupied by Pea Finder near the tepee door.

At early light she was forced awake suddenly and violently by blows from a stick in the hand of See Dead Bull. "Get up!" the woman said. "Get up! You hear me? If you think you are going to sleep all day around here, you can think again. Get outside!"

Outside the woman brandished the stick and said, "Go get some water! Water! You hear me! Can't you understand anything? Water, you fool!"

The girl managed to see the two empty water bags made from horse-leg skins hanging on a rack. She got them loose, dodging most of the blows from See Dead Bull's stick, and escaped to a path.

"Not that way!" the woman yelled. "Water! That way! Don't you understand anything? That way! And it better be clean water. No mud!"

The girl went searching for the water hole along the paths through the trees. Most of the tepees were still quiet. Here and there a solitary woman nursed a fire back to life in the bare space before the door. The most worn paths leading generally downhill obviously went to water holes in the creek. As the girl walked along, she felt the places on her shoulder and hip where she had received the blows.

A dog started barking at her, and soon a half dozen of them were aroused. Most of them stayed near the lodges where they belonged, but persisted in their challenges. She walked straight as if ignoring them. A large gray dog sprang into the path before her, growling and showing his teeth, raising the hair on top of his neck. She turned and deliberately detoured around him.

At the water hole, after carefully filling the bags, she searched in a thicket until she broke loose a limb half as big as her arm and longer than she was tall. She went back with the water and the limb. The dogs began to bark again. When the angry gray dog sprang onto her path, snarling, she carefully leaned the two water bags up against the trunk of a tree. Holding the limb behind her, she walked guardedly forward. The dog crouched and made a fierce face.

Then she sprang. The limb was in front of her in a flash. She swung and caught him, luckily or skillfully, on the point of the nose. The dog tumbled back and made a choking noise, pawing at his bloody face as if to clean the pain from it. The barking from the other dogs stopped suddenly, and all became curiously quiet.

The girl put down the stick, got her water, and proceeded on to the lodge of Antelope Man. Thus she did on her first morning in the camp of her adopted people begin to learn and to assert herself in a humble way. She would not walk between a barking bitch and the place where her pups were hidden. She would not walk between a growling guard dog and the lodge where he belonged. But they had something to learn too. They must let her walk along the public paths of the camp or else suffer from their unpoliteness. Thus she had begun to make for herself a niche, a place to exist, somewhere between the dogs and the human beings.

The women of Antelope Man's lodge had various kinds of sadness and frustration in their pasts. Broken Ice, the mother-in-law, had once been the mistress of a rich lodge. She had borne no son. Of good fortune, there is none like a strong warrior son coming to maturity. But she had two beautiful daughters, who, in another way, are even more valuable. Who can say what might be paid for them in horses or other wealth? And, if daughters made a good marriage in the same band, one keeps the daughters and gains hunter and warrior sons, besides the blessing of grandchildren. Antelope Man had seemed a worthy catch, a man with prospects; but now, though he sat in council as a family head, his voice was not heard much.

It had greatly irritated Broken Ice when Antelope Man had his accident. A horse had stepped on the man's foot. After her own husband had died in a battle with the Lakota, Broken Ice had given her second beautiful daughter to Antelope Man and had joined his lodge, though she brought no horses, for her horse band had been taken by Shoshone raiders. Then Antelope Man got his foot stepped on. Other men get honorable wounds fighting enemies, but what does this one do? He lets a horse step on his foot. The foot swelled up as big as an old-fashioned war club and stayed that

way all through the spring, summer, and autumn
hunting seasons, while the members of the lodge
traded off their wealth in robes and beadwork and
even horses just to put meat on the fire.

The great loss recently, of course, had been the
loss of her grandson. But that tragedy probably hit
See Dead Bull harder than anyone else. The Crow
band had been away up on Elk River, which some
call the Yellowstone, and had tried to cross during
the high spring rise. The roiling muddy water had
been thick with chunks of ice, the rotting half-
frozen carcasses of buffalo, and uprooted timber.
The boys sported recklessly in the crossing, as boys
will, outdaring one another and worrying their
mothers sick. The son of See Dead Bull was among
them, the only child of the lodge. A submerged tree
trunk swept into several horses, crippling some and
making others panic. Two boys were lost that day.
See Dead Bull and Antelope Man found the body
of theirs a long ride downstream in a motte of
willows. His skin was soaked white as a catfish belly. They did not speak his name now.

See Dead Bull was not jealous of her sister,
Birdy, but she was determined that, as first wife,
she should rule the lodge and make hers a proper
decent Crow family. Her husband had said nothing
about his intention of taking a captive on the recent raid, but there was gossip. Word gets around
in a camp. You can find out what's going on, even
when it's secret. She knew that Antelope Man did
not have the highest reputation as a man and a
warrior, but she would not have allowed anyone to
say so in her presence. As for this thing of the Big
Belly, Hairy Nose girl, it was a most outrageous
and ridiculous piece of stupidity. It seemed only

proper and decent that the girl be beaten often and made to work constantly lest anyone imagine for a minute that she was more than a slave. She should be named Slave Girl and that was that.

Birdy was the loving one of the lodge. She was lazy and could not do well at needlework, nor cooking, nor much of anything, but she was pleased at most everything and loved to do small acts of kindness for the others in the lodge. Though she had been married some eight winters to Antelope Man, she still tried to please him; she thought he was the most handsome and brave man alive.

Birdy wished to please her mother and older sister so long as it was not too arduous. If she came sometimes to hit the little captive named Slave Girl with a tree limb, it was not out of meanness or dislike, but merely a perfunctory formal gesture that for some vague reason seemed appropriate.

Pea Finder was the sister of Antelope Man's father, who had been an important man, a Tobacco Planter, in the Crow tribe. She had been married twice briefly: long ago to a young man who died honorably in a battle with the Blackfeet up on Big River, which some call the Missouri; later to a man who had roaming fever. That husband wandered off west so far that he came to a great water, which some call Pacific, and wandered off east so far that he came to a strange land of whites, who have unusual customs and are said to be of the same tribe as white traders. Pea Finger, and indeed her neighbors, had never believed half of what the roaming warrior said on those rare occasions when he came home. Now he had been gone so long that babies born since he left were grown. The earth hold many peculiar people, dangerous to roam among. If that

husband were not killed by now, he would probably be dead of old age anyway.

Pea Finder's old-age name came from a particu-
lar ability she had. She could find caches of peas
better than any other woman who ever lived. In
certain regions of the earth, when times are right,
ground peas bloom and make seeds, almost too
small and scattered for a human being to notice.
But certain small prairie mice gather them, as bees
tediously gather honey, and hoard them in their
nests of sticks and grass built in piles of prickly
pears or dug into sandy banks. A clever woman
may find them by the double handfuls, and they
are tasty food.

Finding peas was the only thing that Pea Finder
was clever at, though she was a good and willing
worker. She was too thin and old to carry much of
a load of wood. She asked for little and got little. If
she learned, as did Birdy, to hit the intruder Slave
Girl, it was only because it seemed proper to do it
sometimes, and not because she felt any malice.

A few days after the raid, the small scabs peeled
off the face of Antelope Man, and one could hardly
see that he had been scratched. Then he went visiting around the village, having a smoke here and
there and telling, with a small laugh, that on the
successful raid he happened to see a good chance to
grab a little female slave, so he did it. She was
worthless, of course, but could help the women
around the tepee.

"Some of the boys laughed at me," he would
say, chuckling. "That's what I love about a raid
party, the good humor. At my age, I have all the
glory and wealth I need, and I only go for the good

fellowship. By the way, did you happen to see my horse herd lately? I guess I'd better go out and locate them and check on them. I have two pregnant mares. Have you heard anything about moving camp? We could get better grazing, I'm sure." Thus he made it clear to the other people of the band that he was not ashamed of his performance on the recent raid. If any gossip was going around the showed him to be ridiculous, it could remain just that, gossip. Some people will gossip; you cannot stop them; you might as well try to stop a hungry bear in a patch of overripe plums.

After he had visited some neighbors, Antelope Man decided that he had neglected his horses too long. He had gotten contradictory information about them from the neighbors. They might be in any direction from camp as far away as a two-hour ride. He informed his womenfolk of his business one morning as he prepared to leave.

Broken Ice said, "I don't see why that husband of yours doesn't try to kill some game. Why should we eat dried meat this time of year?"

He said, "Tell that mother of yours that I shall take my bow. This lodge does not suffer from want of food."

"Tell your husband," she said, "that others have fresh game all the time. I'm not complaining. I can eat anything. But I just wonder what the neighbors think."

In such exchanges, See Dead Bull paid little attention, though supposedly all the words were addressed to her and her sister. Sometimes Birdy tried to relay the messages, but she usually found herself interrupted.

Slave Girl was scraping on a piece of buffalo rawhide, tediously removing the hair and all strings

of hard flesh. As she squatted over her work, she
watched Antelope Man and the women. When he
strode off with his quiver and bow over his shoulder and a lariat rope in his hand, she ran after him.
When he noticed her, she tried to make signs to
him.

"Go back," he said. "You can't go with me."

They were in sight of the tepee, and the women
had seen. See Dead Bull and Broken Ice came after
her, each with a stick, each angry. They were in
reach of Slave Girl before she saw them. She tried
to duck and dodge as they struck her, coming at
her from opposite sides so that she had trouble escaping. They said, "You're going to work! You
hear me! Who do you think you are? You will learn
some sense!"

Antelope Man said, "You don't have to beat her
so much."

Slave Girl, not weeping, but only emitting small
cries of pain when a blow landed, got into the
brush and ran circling toward her work she had left
near the tepee.

Short of breath, Broken Ice said, "I guess that
husband of yours would let her play around all day
and do nothing."

Antelope Man said, "I may decide to have her
help guard the horses, and if I decide that, then I
will do it. I don't want her to be beaten so much."
He turned and walked on.

One day, less than a moon after the successful
raid against the Atsina, the sultry air over the Crow
camp became filled with scurrying clouds. Far to
the west the clouds rose thicker and darker. Distant thunder rumbled.

Those women who were out along the water-

course gathering wood and those on the prairie
digging roots hurried toward the village. Some of
them brought the coals of their cook fires inside
their tepees. Others covered up racks of drying
meat, glancing while they worked toward the
threatening sky and frowning. They let down the
lower flaps of their dwellings and tied them or
weighted them with stones or logs.

They were superstitious people who lived not
only close to nature, but inside nature. Women ran
into the brush and down around the swimming
hole, screaming to their children, "Storm! Storm is
coming! Come to safety! Get inside! Get inside!
Storm!"

As the thunderclouds came near, the whole sky
became a contrast of light and dark movement.
The earth was darkened, her grass and trees jerking
and swaying in the gusty wind. Thunder rumbled.
Lighning flashed erratically. Big drops of rain fell
slanting.

The village was battened down. The last man,
woman, and child had found safety in the lodges as
the prairie storm began to rage overhead. Here and
there a whining dog, which had not been admitted
to safety inside, cowered as near the tepee as he
could. Dogs feel what their people feel. The village
stood desolate, its wet leather and wood glistening
under the lightning.

From the lodge of Antelope Man slipped a
slender human form. It ran with uncertainty in the
direction from which the darker clouds seemed to
be approaching; sometimes it seemed to be shrink-
ing back, sometimes racing boldly.

She ran past the water hole and out onto a broad
flat of sand, jumping with thin arms stretched out,

her face turned up. Though she flinched from the cracks of thunder and the quick chains of lightning, she cried in that queer foreign language of hers—in a high voice with a question and a challenge: "Thunder? Thunder?"

At the edge of the clearing grew tall elm trees, their high limbs sweeping wildly in the wet air. The girl stared with both fear and eagerness all around at the sky. She ran to the tallest tree and began to climb, struggling until she had gone five times as high as a man is tall. She clung with her legs and one hand to the swaying limb and thrust the other thin arm toward the clouds, her face upturned into the whipping rain.

The storms sounds did not cover her words. "Thunder," she prayed, "help me. Please make them like me. Help me, thunder. Make them like me."

3. Stars

Though Slave Girl got many beatings, both light and severe, she could not seem to learn that she must act in a proper and obedient manner. She was never without bruises on arms and legs and back, for she almost daily did some act that annoyed the mistresses of the lodge. Slave Girl would be set to a task, and the next thing they knew, she would have dropped the task entirely and be over under the shade of a tree watching Antelope Man repair the feathers on a bunch of used arrows.

She would try to go to the swimming place with other boys and girls her age and try to go watch them play house or kick ball. Nearly every day the women had to watch her lest she follow Antelope Man when he went hunting or to tend the horses. He did not discourage her as much as they thought he should. Broken Ice often said in his presence, "That husband of yours is going to spoil that stupid slave so she won't be worth a buffalo chip."

One day Antelope Man was making arrowpoints from some pieces of sheet iron he had gotten by trading. He had bent them until they broke into sharp triangles and had pounded them flat. Now, having no file, he had to whet them into final shape and sharpness. He worked at an outcrop of sandstone not far behind his tepee. Slave Girl went to where he sat, took a piece of metal, and began to rub it on the broad rock. He showed her a point he had finished so that she might take it for a pattern.

When See Dead Bull and Broken Ice came with their sticks, he stopped them, saying, "Leave her alone. I want her to help me."

"Tell your husband," said Broken Ice, "that little snip should be working."

"She is working," he said. "Tell your mother Slave Girl is rubbing that iron point on the rock as fast as she can, and exactly the way I told her to."

See Dead Bull put her hands on her hips and accused him. "You are trying to treat her like a daughter instead of a slave."

"I'm not treating her like a daughter. This is not woman's work or girl's work. I just need help. It would take me weeks to do it by myself."

"Tell that husband of yours," said Broken Ice, "that he should hit her sometimes if he expects her to work. She is lazy."

"Tell that mother of yours," he said, "that I will hit her when I get ready, and not before. I want you women to stop beating around on this child so much. If you break her arms or something like that, I'm going to be angry."

See Dead Bull and Broken Ice went back to the tepee. For three full days Slave Girl did no work other than help make iron arrowpoints.

She was learning the language in a limited way, coming to understand the practical meaning of such expressions as these: Go get some water. Go get some wood. Keep the flies off the meat. Scour this pot with sand and wash it well. Turn the meat on the drying racks. Go get more water. Take the small ax and cut some green wood.

One day glad cries rose in the edge of camp. "Chicago! Chicago!" It was mostly children, though some men and women strolled with big grins toward the trail coming in from the east. One chunky woman became more excited; she overturned a cooking pot into the fire, then ran into her tepee to get a porcupine comb, brushed her hair awkwardly without unbraiding it, and put a hasty strip of vermilion paint along the ragged part. She ran out among the children toward the edge of camp, half laughing, half crying. "Chicago! He has come home! Chicago!"

A small caravan approached, one rider leading four loaded pack mules. The rider, dressed in buckskins, was an old man with broad, but humped, shoulders and a ragged gray beard. He was of the type called *masta-cheeda*, a white trader but not French. Now he rode laughing and calling out to the children as they slowed the progress of his horse. Seeing the heavyset, excited woman coming, he slid off his mount and ran to her.

They hugged one another like two dancing bears, trying to lift each other from the ground. She said over and over, "Chicago, my Chicago!"

"Which is ours?" he asked, waving at all the children. "There's the boy! Come here! Let me get hold of you." Soon with her help he had a boy and a girl of three or four years up in his arms.

In a minute he went to one of his pack mules and began to take out of a cloth bag the treat the children had been hoping for—rock candy in yellowish pieces as big as a man's thumb. As he passed it out a piece at a time, he said, "Don't bite it. It will break your teeth. Just hold it in your mouth."

Sometimes he glanced at Slave Girl who was standing at the edge of the group, watching silently. He must have seen the bruises on her arms and neck.

When all the other mouths seemed to be filled, he said to Slave Girl, "Little gal, don't you like candy?"

Perhaps it was his strange appearance that caused her to guess that he must also speak other than Crow. She said in Blackfoot, "I don't know the language well. Do you have a good thing to eat for me?"

In poor Blackfoot he said, "What? What's this? Are you Blackfoot?"

"No, I am Atsina." She changed to that language. "I wanted to find words to speak to you."

She had found the right words. He said, "Atsina! Why I lived with the Big Bellies till they got riled up at me. Little gal, you're smart as a whip! Here. Put this in your mouth, but don't bite it."

"I'm learning Crow," she said. "Antelope Man is my new father."

"You'll learn it," he said. "If you ever want to know a word, ask me. *En passant, parlez-vous français?*"

"*No,*" she said. "*No comprendo. Pero, hablo español poco—poquito.*"

"Bless my soul!" he said in Crow. "I'm dumbfounded! Flabbergasted! Little gal, you got a brain in your head! Bless my Goddamn rusty soul, I think you're talking Spanish. I never saw the like, white ner red. You talk in good Blackfoot and Atsina. You don't speak no French, but you know what I say. Then you talk to me in words I don't know, but still I understand."

She was rolling the hard piece of candy around in her mouth, clamping her lips to keep the sweet juice from leaking.

He asked, "Did you hurt your arms and legs?"

She sucked in and swallowed and answered in poor Crow, "I think I fell down."

"I think you must of rolled down a long bank. Listen, little gal, don't worry none about learning Crow. You will talk to them, that's for sure. You ever want any help with words, come to me. I got to go and take care of my business now, but you come and ask me. You're smart as a whip!"

He waved the cloth candy bag at the children to show them it was empty, then led his pack animals to the tepee of his wife. Later he took presents of hunting knives to the principal civil chief High Owl and to other important men such as Elk Head, Rainy, and One Good Eye. Gossip around the camp said that Chicago was in trouble with white people, that he refused to trade with any Crow enemies, and that he might stay with the band a year or more before going on another trading trip.

Slave Girl had taken an interest in Antelope Man's bow and arrows. They hung sometimes in a place of honor on the tepee wall, at other times along with the master's shield on a small tripod outside to absorb the magic of sunlight. Slave Girl would be found standing near them, staring intently, sometimes moving around to get a better look.

Broken Ice would say, "What are you doing, Slave Girl? Get away from there!"

And See Dead Bull would say, "If you ever

touch those things, you'll wish you hadn't! Have you no respect?"

It was over the bow and arrows that Slave Girl got her worst beating. Both Broken Ice and See Dead Bull were gone from the lodge most of the day.

Broken Ice was a lodge skin cutter. In fact, she was a person who knew how to supervise a half dozen women in the making of a tepee; however, the skill of cutting a dozen or more tanned buffalo hides to fit together properly was so important that they called such a woman the cutter. When the first wife of a lodge had decided that her tepee had become shabby and she had gathered the necessary hides and sinew and thongs, she would invite a few good-working friends and a cutter to an all-day party. The women would eat and chat and work under the advice of the cutter. Broken Ice, knowing that age was creeping up on her, was slowly giving her valuable knowledge to her eldest daughter.

On this day, Broken Ice, having received a present of twenty polished elk teeth and a long iron spoon, had agreed to serve as cutter at a lodge across camp. She and See Dead Bull left early. Antelope Man left to spend the day with the horses; he was watching for a new colt. Birdy took advantage of the situation to sleep most of the day. Pea Finder wandered out in the brush humming to herself.

The weapons of Antelope Man hung on their small tripod. It would be the duty of See Dead Bull to take them inside at sundown, or earlier if the sky became cloudy. Slave Girl had been left to pound some dried meat, with a stern warning not to get any sand on it. The incorrigible girl, finding herself unwatched, soon dropped her work and went to study the bow and quiver of arrows.

Soon she begun to touch the forbidden equipment, feeling the feathers and their binding on the arrows. Then she took one of the seven arrows out to feel its heft and balance. After a minute she began to try to string the bow and finally succeeded by bearing all her weight on the upper end. No one else was stirring around the lodge. Slave Girl took the bow and quiver of arrows in her arms and headed out of the village, past the toilet place, to a secluded area among the trees. She begun to play with them, shooting at the trunks of trees.

Being a hunting and warrior people, the Crows gave considerable importance to a man's weapons. They were rarely loaned or borrowed. Only a first wife could handle them, and not even she during the days once each moon when a woman is sick.

About midday Antelope Man came home for a bite to eat. Seeing his weapons missing, he asked Birdy about them. She quickly located Pea Finder, who scurried across camp to give the shocking news to Broken Ice and See Dead Bull. They ran back home and, guessing the truth, began to scream for Slave Girl.

"That little fool has gone too far this time," See Dead Bull said.

"Tell your husband," said Broken Ice, "that she should be killed for this."

The four women found sticks and limbs and headed out of camp to search. Soon Pea Finder met the guilty child, who had heard the commotion and was trying to bring back the weapons. Pea Finder screamed for the others. The four women converged on Slave Girl and began swinging at her.

Broken Ice and See Dead Bull cut her off each time she tried to escape. A solid blow to the neck knocked her to the ground. She cowered there, trying to shield her face, and began to cry.

Antelope Man approached and said, "That's enough! Stop hitting her! Do you hear me? When I say stop, I mean stop."

He picked up his bow and quiver and said, "You've got her to bleeding. You beat her too much."

The women were breathless. See Dead Bull said, "She's ruined your weapons."

"They are not hurt," he said.

Slave Girl, wracked with deep sobs, would not look up at them.

Broken Ice said, "I hope your husband knows what a disgrace this is. We are the instructors and guides at a tepee cutting, but we have to waste time hunting a little slave and thief. What will the neighbors think?"

"Tell your mother to go back and leave her alone," he said.

That afternoon the activity around the lodge was strange. Broken Ice and See Dead Bull went back to their work party across camp. Pea Finder and Birdy took up the dry-meat pounding job of Slave Girl, sometimes glancing out in the direction where the beaten child lay. Antelope Man paced back and forth saying nothing.

Finally he strode back out that way. Birdy and Pea Finder sneaked after him to see what he would do. He did nothing except go near where the girl cowered in the grass, stand a while, scratch his head, then return to camp. But after some time he again went out there, and Birdy and Pea Finder covertly followed. He went near the girl, cleared his throat, and said, "It's all right."

She looked up. Her eyes were red and dark from rubbing.

He turned around a few times, said, "Well . . . ," then said, "Don't ever do it again unless you ask me."

Later, as night approached, Birdy took the girl a horn of rich broth.

Slave Girl did not come to the tepee to sleep, but at the first sign of dawn she limped into camp and took the horse-leg water bags to carry a morning supply of water for the lodge.

It was that kind of late summer weather when heat waves tremble over the plains and old buffalo bulls, driven from their herds by younger males, travel alone and angry, with dry froth hanging from their mouths. Along the watercourses, birds flocked around the pockets of tepid water. High Owl's band of Absarokas decided to break camp and head for a mountain valley where it would be cooler.

That morning the village was bustling before sunrise. The women of Antelope Man's lodge put on their best dresses, then dismantled the tepee. Everything else was already packed. Kettles, pots, pans, extra clothing, food, tools, and all such were put in leather bags or rawhide boxes to be hung from pack saddles. When Antelope Man brought in the horses, the tepee cover, carefully folded, was loaded on one. The women made a travois of two lodgepoles for Pea Finder to ride on along with a number of hides and robes. The other women rode pack horses. Antelope Man carried nothing on his horse except his bow and quiver, for as a warrior he needed to be always ready when traveling and also had to tend the unused horses.

The women took pride in being able to break camp quickly. See Dead Bull was satisfied that only about half the band had begun to trek west when her household was loaded and ready. No one told Slave Girl where she should ride, so she mounted the bony old gray without a bridle. Antelope Man gave her a short hair rope, which, being looped about the animal's neck and set in a half hitch around his nose, served to guide him.

Antelope had trouble getting his horses out of camp and into the line of travel. Ten of them carried either riders or other loads; the other ten, besides two new colts, ran free. Soon Slave Girl began to help herd them, cutting off those that tried to go their own ways and patiently urging on those that wanted to stop and graze.

The moving camp presented a gay and lively appearance as it stretched out on the plains. Since it is easier to take care of fancy dress and decorations by wearing them than by packing them, and since everyone would be in plain sight of everyone else, many people wore their best. Men wore ermine wraps on their hair or as leggings, also wrappings of scarlet cloth and feathers in their hair. Some wore jewelry of silver or sea shells, traded from the far west or far east. Women wore dresses of fine doeskin or the skins of bighorn sheep, chalked white and decorated with elk teeth or bright beads or porcupine quills. Colorful scarves and shawls were much in evidence, as well as blankets of cotton and wool, some traded from far south and made by a people called Navaho. The horses wore feathers on their bridles and in their manes. They were fat and spirited. Young men and women added to the festive air by showing off and flirting with one another.

Far ahead of the long procession rode three wolves. The Fox Society of warriors supervised the movement, but all the men aided in guarding, each one riding now and then out to a high point to the side. On occasions when Antelope Man left the procession, Slave Girl found herself driving his band of free horses. She cut herself a small switch to aid in urging on her mount and she yelled at her charges as the men and boys who were herding sometimes did.

When they came to water for a camp the sun was setting. She held the free horses while Antelope Man helped unpack and drive out the others. He spoke to a Fox Society man and volunteered to serve a short token guard. After hobbling two lead mares, he said to Slave Girl, "Go eat and sleep."

"I want to go with you," she said.

He said nothing, so she rode after him up to the crest of a ridge, where they dismounted and sat down to watch darkness coming over the land.

They could see the area of the temporary camp. Here and there a campfire started. Some men and some women took pride in being fire starters. They struck flint against steel or twirled a drilling stick in their hands and caught the sparks or heat in fine rubbed dry grass. The more successful ones usually sprinkled a few grains of gunpowder in their dry grass. Most of the people borrowed fire. Much good-natured teasing went on. "Cannot get a fire started, hey? It takes skill. Here, take a few coals!" It was a matter for joking, but also an honor to start fire. Fire starters would brag: "Fourteen lodges have borrowed my fire."

From where Slave Girl and Antelope Man sat on the ridge, the camp was a distant vision. They could hear some faint peals of laughter or shouting, could see the red-yellow points of fire starting along the string of the night camp. They sat silently as the Earth Mother unrolled her robe of darkness, and the stars began to shine down their pricks of light.

Suddenly Antelope Man said: "I was teaching my boy about the stars. He was smart. If you were a boy, I would teach you."

They could hear their two mounts cropping grass, snorting gently now and then to blow the dust from their nostrils.

"You see, the stars are important," he said. "That one up there is the star that does not move. It's not the brightest, but all the others go around it. In traveling, that star is very good to find your way, so that you go straight. If you were a boy, I would explain it to you.

"See over there. We call it Seven Stars and it makes a dipper. See the square bowl and the bended handle? Now, the two stars at the end of the square bowl, they point at the star that does not move. See where the dipper is? If you look just at dark, it is at a certain place and it goes halfway around during the night, before the sun fades the stars. You can tell how much night has passed.

"I wish you were a boy, for I like to tell my knowledge and explain these important things. I have learned from my father, and I have also observed on my own."

She stared at the heavens and at him, gripping

her small fists, then pointing in a small manner where he pointed with a grand gesture.

"You see, all the stars go around the one that does not move. Those farther away make a bigger circle. Much can be seen from looking and knowing. If we moved that way up toward Big River, the star that does not move would rise higher in the sky. Thus we can tell where we are by looking at the night. *Maga-hawathus*, he made all things. He made it for us to see and know and use. *Napa* helped him place the stars so that we can understand. So we can tell where we are, how to go straight, and how much night has passed.

"But there is more. I would tell you if you were a boy. You see, the dipper was right there when the sun went down. That's because we are approaching the Moon when Sweet Plums Fall. If we wait till the Moon when Sage Hens Dance, then the dipper will be over there when the sun turns it loose. Thus we can tell the season of the year by looking at the sky.

"But there is more. See that bright one that does not twinkle? I call those foolers or wanderers. They were set up there by Old Man Coyote. And you know how he is. They do not wait in fixed patterns like other stars; they go around and try to fool you. Old Man Coyote, he is all right. *Maga-hawathus*, he lets him do that. The wandering stars—watch out for them—but they are for beauty and for change and to keep us smart, to see how they move over the fixed patterns. Do you understand?"

"Yes, Father," she said.

"Where is the star that does not move?"

"That one. Right there."

"Which way does the dipper go round?"

"That way. Over like that. It will be way over there just before the sun comes up."

"That's right. You don't speak too well, and you don't pronounce right, but I believe you understand. What would happen if we went up on Big River?"

"The star that does not move would rise. If we went away up among the Blackfeet, it would rise way up."

"What if we went down that way among the Shoshone?"

"It would get lower, but all would go around it still."

"That's right. But what is that bright one over there?"

"It's a wanderer, Father. Old Man Coyote sent it for a trick. But it is for beauty and change and to keep us smart."

"You understand," he said. "However, you really don't talk too well. If you want to know a word or how to say it, ask me. I will tell you."

They sat some minutes listening to the faraway calls of the guards around the temporary camp. Antelope Man rose, cupped his hands to his mouth, and made a howl like a wolf.

Not long afterward he rose again and said, "Let's go eat and sleep, Horse Tender. We have work to do tomorrow."

He had not objected when she called him father; now he had called her a new name. The name Horse Tender meant that for him she was no longer a slave, but as for the others of his lodge, that would be a different matter.

4. Horse Tender

High Owl's band of Crows moved several times each year—to find better hunting or grazing; to gather chokecherries or serviceberries or plums when they ripened; to find a cooler campsite in late summer or to find a low protected valley with plenty of firewood in the time of snow and bitter north wind. Customarily they met in spring with other Crow bands for a traditional tobacco planting ceremony, then early in the summer for the Sun Dance. Sometimes they moved far up on the headwaters of the Yellowstone, from whence trading parties would go farther west to barter with the Nez Percé or other tribes, giving dried meat and robes for horses and Spanish horse gear.

Horse Tender took advantage of the fact that there was only one man in the lodge in order to escape from some of the women's work she had been doing. At the slightest excuse she would go out and tend the horses, sometimes asking Antelope Man such a question as, "Should I go see how far away the horse herd is? The big paint gelding was lame a little, you know."

He would say, "I guess so. Yes, go see."

And she would say, "If he's still lame, I could

bring him in and let you look at his foot. He might
have a stone or a thorn in it."

"Yes, bring him in if he limps."

Antelope Man found her a considerable help. By
the time she had lived with the Crows one year, she
was spending only half her time as a slave to the
women; the other half was spent in the relative
freedom of tending horses. Broken Ice and See
Dead Bull resented it. The girl tried to have her
way as much as possible, but also tried to be
diplomatic; in the sight of the women she rode only
the bony gray; away from camp she rode every
horse Antelope Man owned, even some untended
horses belonging to other families. If she were
walking out to find her own band, she often borrowed an unwatched strange horse, rode him, and
later took him back where she had found him.

While tending horses she met a friendly boy
about her own age, Ride Away. He proudly
showed her a bruise on his arm and bragged that he
had got it from breaking wild horses to ride. She
showed him the bruises on her arms and legs and
neck, which she had gotten from beatings, and said
that she too had been riding wild horses. Ride
Away believed the lie, for Horse Tender obviously
rode well.

Sometimes they raced their mounts. Other times
they sat together to eat the lunches they had
brought, of dried meat or pemmican made of meat
and berries and marrow fat.

In that second autumn, High Owl's band of
Crows camped on Thick Ash Tree Creek. Antelope
Man got interested in making a supply of arrows,
for he had found a field of serviceberry brush,
which sometimes grows sprouts of just the right

size. When the sap goes down but before hard freezing weather—that is the time to cut arrows.

The warrior searches and selects carefully the shafts for straightness and size. He binds them together in a bundle with wet rawhide thong, taking care that any natural curve in each small limb is straightened by the strength of the entire bundle. He hangs the bundle inside the tepee beneath the smoke hole so that the wood may cure. Then during long winter days he can straighten each shaft perfectly by applying heat and stress, can smooth it by rubbing it through a sandstone with a groove or a hole in it.

Antelope Man had hung his bundle to cure in the smoke. One evening shortly before sundown when the family members stood or squatted before the tepee, See Dead Bull asked her husband, "When did you get the second bundle of arrow shafts?"

"I have one. It's hanging up in there."

"You have two."

"I have only one bundle. It's hanging up in there, plain as day."

See Dead Bull ducked into the tepee door in an angry manner. Shortly she came out with a bundle of cut sticks. She said, "That filthy Slave Girl has done this! Now she is trying to take over the lodge!" She threw the bundle into the campfire.

Antelope Man sprang to his feet. The tied package of perhaps forty sticks looked much like the one he had put together. He swung wildly and kicked the bundle out of the fire, scattering coals in every direction. He rolled the bundle over with his moccasin a few times, then asked Horse Tender, "Did you cut these?"

"Yes." She had retreated a little way and stood ready to run if one of the women came toward her with a stick.

They went around stamping out small fires, which had started in the dry leaves, temporarily silenced by Antelope Man's violent display.

Finally Broken Ice said, "Tell your husband that Slave Girl wasted time cutting those things when she should have been working."

"Tell your mother," he said, "that maybe Horse Tender has some spare time while the horses are drinking and such. These are good shafts. First class. I can use them."

"Tell your husband that this dirty girl is treated more like a member of the family than like a slave. What will the neighbors think?"

"Tell your mother that the neighbors will think I beat my wives if I don't get a little more respect around here. I'm going to hang this bundle back in the smoke hole, and if anyone touches it without my permission, they'll answer to me."

That winter he worked on arrows by the dim fire in the tepee while the snow and ice came down from the north to grip their cold fingers on the Earth Mother. Horse Tender watched him. With much labor, he had bored a small hole in a rock as large as two fists, using a twirling stick and sand. He showed her how to reduce the roughness and heaviness of an arrow shaft by drawing it through the hole.

It was a cold winter and she spent long hours bringing cottonwood bark and sprouts to feed three or four of Antelope Man's favorite horses.

It was the time of year when prairie turnips, or

pomme blanc, were ripe for digging across the plains, and Horse Tender had been sent with Pea Finder to join Birdy in the digging of food. Pea Finder did not go where the other women were scattered out, but began to search along the sandy banks of a dry wash. The two carried tough pieces of chokecherry limb, sharpened at one end, and Pea Finder went along poking around in the sand and in clumps of grass.

"The diggers are out that way," Horse Tender said. "See away over there?"

"Peas are better," Pea Finder said.

"But there are no peas. Everyone says this is not the right place or the right time of year. You said it yourself."

"Maybe there are peas and maybe there are not peas," the old woman said.

Near the dry gully grew piles of prickly pear, their thick gray-green leaves studded with long thorns and short fine thorns. Later their red fruit, tuna, would make food for coyotes and wolves and also Indians. Some of the piles had been made into small fortresses with sticks and grass and buffalo chips nestled among the thorns; here mice had built their homes safe from the sniffing of predators. Pea Finder poked into these nest piles with her digging stick, saying in a high voice: "Mouse! mouse! mouse!"

Horse Tender said, "If we don't bring home some prairie turnips, I will get a beating."

"Peas are better. Mouse! mouse! mouse!" The old woman bent her face down near the ground and peered intently. "I cannot tell whether it's mouse tracks or lizard tracks. Mouse! mouse! mouse!"

"I will get a beating. Let's go find Birdy."

As Pea Finder prowled along the dry wash and Horse Tender waited with her digging stick and empty leather bag, a horseman approached, the trader Chicago, a hulk of a man, always smiling. His five-year-old son sat before him on the horse and held the reins.

"Hello," he said. "My boy is taking me for a ride."

He got down and said, "Little gal, you're growing. Before we know it, you'll be a woman. Sometime I want to talk to you and sharpen up my Blackfeet talk and my Atsina."

To the boy he said, "Let him graze awhile. Give him a little rein."

Horse Tender said, "We are sent to dig prairie turnips, but we are in the wrong place."

He said to Pea Finder, "I knew your brother well. He was a good Crow leader. Me and him used to go to the Mandan village to trade."

"He was like me," the old woman said. "We are hunting peas, which is the best food. The mice creatures cache them and I find them. I am good at it."

Chicago existed outside their habits and values and ways and ceremonies. He was not tied to those things by training in childhood. and the Crows understood it. He was valuable to them, as liaison to other tribes and the distant whites, as a supplier of iron tools; yet he was more than all that. He was free to talk to children and slaves and mighty chiefs, free to love his fat wife and two children, free to laugh; and Indian people love laughter. Strangely, they never even asked the question whether he was brave.

"Did you find any peas?" he asked.

She held out her gnarled hand with three little peas in it. "This is not a good place."

"Why do you hunt?"

"Peas are good," she said. "I'm the best to find them, because I see them. I see the mice running on the land in my dreams. They fill their jaws and spit them into a pile in their homes."

Horse Tender said, "This is not a good place to dig prairie turnips. I will get a beating when we go home."

Chicago asked, "If you know you cannot find peas here, how come you try to find peas here?"

"They are good to eat," Pea Finder said. "Do you know the greatest cache ever found, over on a creek that runs into Bighorn River? I was a young woman. I looked at mouse tracks and I found the cache. I dug and dug. It was so much peas, you wouldn't believe it. Three women got their bags full and it was all they could carry."

"You are a genius," Chicago said. "No I believe it. Bless my rusty soul. Now, you should go out there where the other women are digging."

Pea Finder said, "It was a big find. They talked about it. Three families ate them all through the winter."

"You're the champion," he said. "Now, you take Horse Tender and go over yonder and dig turnips. See, away over there?"

All she had wanted was to prove her competence. She said, "All right," and to Horse Tender, "Come on, Slave Girl." As they walked away she said, "That man is nice. He understands things. Not just me, but he didn't want you to get a beating. Isn't he nice?"

Horse Tender stopped and put her hands on her little hips and asserted, "Don't you hit me anymore."

Pea Finder seemed surprised at this unusual statement. "You mean today?"

"I mean not any more at all."

"Why?"

"Because it hurts me and I don't want you to do it."

"But I don't hit you hard."

"I don't want you to do it anyway."

"Why?"

"Because it hurts my feelings."

"Oh."

They walked in silence. Pea Finder's sharp shoulder blades stuck out behind her humped back like the wing bones of some skinny bird of prey. She sniffed a couple of times.

"I'll go back with you," Horse Tender said, "and hunt peas if you want to."

"Will you go with me sometime in autumn on a good prairie where we can find some?"

"Yes."

"Will you let me teach you? And listen when I tell you how to find them?"

"Yes."

"All right. There's Birdy over there. Come on. It's stupid to hunt peas right now."

Birdy was working and sweating, her bag half full. Pea Finder went up close to her and began to whisper. They glanced at Horse Tender frequently as they whispered; one might have thought they discussed the unusual request not to be hit. Finally, Birdy, who was given to direct and simple expressions, came over and said, "Horse Tender, we love you."

They had fun that day on the prairie singing a small girl's song:

"Feed me. Feed me.
"Dig in the ground.
"Fill up your carry bag,
"And don't fall down."

Over and over they sang it, laughing because it was so unimportant and because it was for little girls. When they paused in their work, laid down bags and digging sticks, and went to a water hole for a drink, they put their arms around each other's waists like three sisters. They could not skip well because Pea Finder's legs were stiff, but she giggled about it along with them.

Not long past midday they got hungry and started home. Again they sang the silly song:

"Feed me. Feed me.
"Dig in the ground.
"Fill up your carry bag,
"And don't fall down."

Then without discussing the matter or explaining it, each of the older women put handfuls of their roots in the girl's bag, enough to fill it. It was an unspoken conspiracy; the two older ones could not be beaten. After this day, Pea Finder and Birdy called the captive by the name of Horse Tender whenever Broken Ice and See Dead Bull were not present.

Also they helped her make clothes for herself. They could claim a share of trading cloth or tanned doeskin and they supplied it freely. Neither Pea Finder nor Birdy was much of a seamstress, but at least she no longer had to wear cast-off rags that did not fit.

That autumn when the leaves had been frostbitten and had turned red and tan and yellow, Antelope Man went west with a trading party to meet the Nez Percé and Shoshonis. The Crows took all manner of handicrafts, but mostly pack loads of dried buffalo meat and tanned skins of animals, with and without the hair.

Antelope Man returned in a fortnight with much good property, first a large spirited black mare that was about to foal; then seventeen long new lodgepoles, straight and thin and strong; then some junk property such as a worn cradle board and several baskets woven of cattail fibers; then jewelry. To Broken Ice and Pea Finder he gave necklaces of sea shells. To his first wife See Dead Bull, a string of bright southern beans and turquoise stones. To his second wife Birdy, a small silver cross on a silver chain.

Then he said, "Oh, I almost forgot. A Nez Percé man had this half-bow for his son, but the boy outgrew it, so the man gave it to me. I give it to Horse Tender. It's not much good, but she can play with it while she's watching the horses or such."

He said to her sternly, "Here! Now don't you play with this toy when you're supposed to be working or you will have to answer to me."

He handed her a bow as long as she was tall, the most beautifully made bow that any of them had ever seen, along with eight arrows. The women became quiet, staring. The girl held the gift in her two hands, like something precious that might drop and break. Broken Ice and See Dead Bull seemed about to speak, but Antelope Man quickly continued:

"Now, I want you to listen to me, little girl! I'm the head of this lodge and I can be a hard man. Don't you ever forget it. That bow is not much good, though it's all right for a free gift; but you better understand. If a new baby is born in this lodge from one of my wives, that baby gets the bow, for you are only a slave. You better thank these good women for your luck where you get to eat our food and sleep in our tepee. Don't you ever forget it."

He got away with his lie by talking fast. "Now, I want you to take your toy and get out there and take care of my new mare. You pay attention or you'll get in trouble. That mare is bred to the fastest race horse in the whole Nez Percé nation. They are great breeders. Even the Shoshonis say so. The studhorse that bred her won every race they put him in. That's a good mare; she's a warhorse herself. I want you to take her out and put her with my herd and make sure she settles down and the others don't fight her. You see to it. Get going! You better watch your step and do right and don't complain or you'll be in trouble."

She had been raising up and down on her toes, waiting for him to stop talking. She turned and went out toward the picketed mare. Birdy and Pea Finder ran after her to look at the bow.

It was not a toy, not really a half-bow; it's pull made it a full woman's bow. Antelope Man had traded for it five soft buffalo robes and enough dried meat to feed a family one winter. The bow was made of sections of sheep's horn overlapping, glued with hard hoof-glue, the whole cut and

scraped and polished, smooth black and blending
gray and clear. It was a double-curved bow, so that
its center came near the string of twisted sinew. Of
the arrows four were tipped with flint and four
with sharp iron.

In the days following, the fading middle-aged
warrior and the girl in puberty looked at one another across a cook fire or a hard-packed lodge
yard. He was like a father who says, "If a man
comes to her he'd better treat her right or I will kill
him; yet how childish she still is!" She was like a
girl saying, "My father loves me and he is like the
sun, with all power and wisdom; my heart will go
anywhere with him and the great, glorious world is
open before me." Perhaps what their eyes said was
more simple: "Thank you, father," and "It's all
right; be careful, daughter."

She presided in the snow at the birth of the colt.
She brought a pot of water, which the mare would
not drink. The big black mother, whose body heat
had melted the snow in a wallow under the bank,
looked with her large eyes at Horse Tender. The
girl helped get out the gutlike afterbirth, then tried
to help the awkward, knobby-kneed baby. That's
why it had been so hard, because he was so big. She
deposited him like a pile of crooked wood under
the muzzle of his anxious mother.

The newborn had a voracious appetite and she
first put the mare's tit in his mouth. Horse Tender
packed in cottonwood bark and dug-out grass for
the mother. She picked up the colt a hundred times
and stood him back on his clumsy legs. She dug
him out of snowbanks. She raced him in the hoof-
deep snow, laughing at him and his stub tail, which
he held straight up. The colt thought she was his

other mother or perhaps his sister or perhaps his god.

Horse Tender and Ride Away pondered a name for him and decided on Smoke, for his coat was fully as black as that of his mother, but not so shiny. Antelope Man agreed to the name. He said it was the friskiest baby studhorse he had ever seen.

Horse Tender was filling out and growing like a wild weed. Also, stories and attitudes about her, strange ideas, were growing; but only among the weakest and most innocent and least influential of the Crow band.

The naked children knew her. Girls of three or four and boys a year or two older, who went without clothes in warm weather, stopped their play when she passed by, because of the way she walked or rode or because of what they had heard in some kind of underground childish gossip. They called her indiscriminately Slave Girl or Horse Tender.

Some of the older children knew a little more. One boy tried to take an arrow she had shot. He went home with a bloody nose. Because of pride, he could not say what had happened to him, so he said he fell off a cliff.

Ride Away knew well that she won horse races against him as often as she lost, that she could run as fast as he, that she knew the woods and prairie at least as well. But of what value is the opinion of one barely entering manhood, who has never counted coup or stolen an enemy horse?

In the band lived two men called *berdaches,* cowards who admit they are cowards. They did the work of women. Whether they were sexually attracted to men or to women seemed not an impor-

tant issue; they simply had refused ever to take on
the violent and dangerous duties of hunter and
warrior. Their opinions were of little value, and no
one of importance would speak to them. They
added to the growing underground rumors, saying
that Horse Tender was an unusual person for one
so young, a person to be watched.

Chicago did not know what to think about her.
He was amazed that she had learned Absaroka
speech so fully so quickly. As far as he could judge,
she spoke perfect Atsina and perfect Blackfoot.
When he spoke to her in French, she understood.
He had begun to teach her some English words,
and she never forgot a word after hearing it once.
She said English words like "water," "fire,"
"tree," "dog," and "food" with a Crow accent; but
what startled him was that if she had been speaking
Atsina, she said the English words with an Atsina
accent; and if he had been speaking French to her,
she said English words with a French accent. What
kind of sense does that make?

Equally intriguing was the matter of her shooting with bow and arrow. One day Chicago met her
near the village, and she said she was hunting for
squirrels. A practical man, he explained that a
hunter cannot get squirrels alone. No one can hit
them when they bound along a branch or spring
from one tree to another. They stop on the trunk,
but they hide on the other side. It takes two hunters
to stand on opposite sides. She seemed to listen
carefully, but later that day she delivered to his
wife four fresh, cleaned squirrels as a gift.

Antelope Man was confused about her. He loved
the girl as if she were a daughter and was pleasantly
surprised at how much she helped him. She

brought him feathers of the crane, duck, wood-peacker, owl, hawk. She would babble theories about weapons when they could talk alone. "Father, some arrows are not feathered right. You can see an arrow go round when you shoot it. I think on every wing of a bird are three feathers, a single wing, and they belong together on one shaft. They are curved the same. If they are mixed up, right wing and left wing, or from two birds, then they go in a kind of looping flight. They go like a shaft not straight enough, and not exactly true. Don't you think so?"

He would say, "Yes, that's probably true."

But how did she know it? He knew she must be a good shot, for she brought in dressed ducks and rabbits and squirrels. And where did she get all those feathers she brought him? He did not believe the other rumor about her, that she rode horses from his and others' herds—horses that had never yet been broke and trained to carry a rider.

5. Smoke

A Crow camp was a continual training place, a school for the generation leaving childhood and looking forward to the myriad privileges and duties of adulthood. Some of the teen-agers looked ahead eagerly to being grown; others felt more timid. Boldness was encouraged among the boys. While the girls were taught quietly and privately, the boys were taught in gangs with fanfare.

Council members and leaders of warrior societies sponsored and supervised competitions for boys and young men: horse races, foot races, shooting with the bow at a rolling hoop, the breaking of horses, games of stealth where pieces of meat were stolen from the lodges of their own camp.

High Owl's band had camped on the south bank of Elk River, just above the high-water line, near another Crow band of some sixty lodges, which had camped on lower ground. The leading men had chosen the location because of a good area of backwater, chest-deep, perfect for breaking horses. Daily they brought unbroken stock from one of the camps, a few at a time, and herded them against the water. Young men took them out to a depth so that they could not buck effectively and made them accustomed to the weight of a pack or rider. Young men such as Ride Away took it for a sport. Men, women, and children took it for a show; always some stood back on the high ground watching. Horse owners took it for a useful, even necessary, activity.

Now a year and a half old but still called a yearling, Antelope Man's colt Smoke was larger than most horses his age. He looked mature, when he was not playing wildly, running, kicking at imaginary wolves and panthers.

Antelope Man told Horse Tender to bring the yearling to the horse breakers.

"Do we have to?" she asked.

"We sure do. He's plenty big. If he can be trained, he will make a great racehorse and warhorse and buffalo horse."

"I think he's already tame," she said.

The women had been puttering around the front of the lodge, but now stopped to listen.

Horse Tender said, "I mean I don't think Smoke will like it. I'll go bring him, but he's already tame."

See Dead Bull said, "Now she's trying to take over the horse herd."

Antelope Man laughed. "He's the wildest horse around here."

"I'll go get him," Horse Tender said, "but I don't think it's fair. Out in the water that way, and a stranger jumps on your back."

"Tell your husband," said Broken Ice, "that it's a shame and a disgrace the way he let's that girl sass him."

The mother-in-law and her eldest daughter no longer beat the girl, since she was bringing in small game and doing most of the horse herding, but they were unbending in their opposition to considering the girl a member of the family. Antelope Man tried to laugh off the differences that arose.

Horse Tender went to her task, riding one of the older saddle horses. She threw Smoke in with the small herd of young horses about midday. The young men got to him in the middle of the afternoon. Ride Away, who had been taking his turn at riding the plunging wild stock, acted strangely. He backed away and finally joined the spectators.

They fought the yearling until they had fastened a hackamore about his head, but he seemed determined not to enter the water. They surrounded him with mounted riders, two at the rear, then shoved and crowded him out. The deeper they went, the more Smoke struggled. When the water came upon his belly, a daring young man sprang from another horse onto his back.

The yearling exploded, as will certain damp stones in a campfire. The two dozen or so spectators yelled, but they could see little because of the splashing, churning white water. They saw horses' legs and men's legs stuck briefly up toward the sky and there were equally brief periods when most of the men and animals were out of sight under swirling water. Smoke came out of it alone and headed away from the bank, out into the broad, shiny current of the river.

Someone said, "There's an outlaw horse if I ever saw one."

Another said, "He won't stop this side of Blackfoot country."

Horse Tender ran from among the spectators and into the water downstream of the horse-break-

ing area. She swam into the current after the horse.
Antelope Man and Ride Away ran to the water's
edge and shouted, but she would not turn back.

The spectators helped get the young horse
breakers and their mounts out of the water. One
horse had a broken leg. The five young men who
had been in the water were bruised; one had a broken arm, already swelling, ugly blue, as if blood
veins were crushed.

The watchers who looked at the river could see
the head and neck of the black horse, trailing a
wake like that of a boat, and the smaller black head
of the young woman, bobbing on the tide. At this
point the swirling water was about the span of a
long arrow flight. They drifted downstream faster
than they made headway across.

Antelope Man, feeling responsible, quickly went
to camp and hired the services of a medicine man
to care for the broken arm. He was contemplating
taking his best swimming horse and crossing to the
north of the river, but this possibility was taken
from him, for the two Crow camps suddenly realized an unsuspected condition, which made them
forget the horse-breaking accident. The river was
rising.

Elk River, which had been called *La Roche
Jaune* by the whites and was now called Yellowstone by such *mastacheeda* as Chicago, headed far
to the west on the continental divide. A thousand
creeks and tiny streams made up the headwaters.
In part of the area, geysers spouted water out of the
earth and water lay in pools as clear as air, with
blue-green rocks on the bottom. Some of the water
was hot enough to cook meat. But the critical fact
at this time was the melting of snowdrifts in that

high country. The Crow camps had paid no attention to the bank of clouds that lay far up on the western horizon the day before. A heavy warm rain had fallen on the headwaters. Much snow was stacked in drifts deeper than a man is tall. It began to melt, then to slide off in great slushy chunks, to feed what had been small streams. The water fed the thousand tributaries and rushed down to the Yellowstone.

The river swelled. It tore off muddy banks and undermined trees and brush and grass, which fell into its torrent and were swept down as a constant stream of debris. The river unseated boulders in its bed and rolled them along. The muddy water cut new channels through deep beds of gravel and sand.

At first in the lower camp the Crows nearest the water began to strike their tepees and carry property to higher ground. Then all in that camp fell in to help. As the water rose, High Owl's people began to help. They could not stay ahead of the swelling river; one family would be slogging through the shallows to help others rescue their gear, then suddenly see the water lapping at their own tepee door.

They built bonfires to light their work during the night. About half of the lodgepoles and covers of the lower camp were saved. Much dried food and other property was lost. All of them appreciated the wisdom of the leaders of High Owl's band in selecting a campsite above the highwater line. Next morning they saw that the river was five times as wide as normal, still rushing madly, still carrying in its muddy currents the debris it had torn loose.

In the afternoon of that day Antelope Man sat alone on a rock some distance from camp. He was looking at the sky and the land to the north, thinking about the boy who now would have been a young man, about the little girl who had so quickly matured into a beautiful young woman. He did not want to be around other people and talk to them. The day seemed unreal to him.

A voice said, "Father, are you asleep?"

He thought he was probably dreaming or having a vision, but it sounded exactly like Horse Tender.

"Father, are you awake?"

She was standing there holding some knotted hair rope.

"Here's the hackamore, Father. I guess it belongs to one of the young men."

He found his voice and asked, "How did you cross the river?"

"It was not too hard to swim over there, but the current took me downstream."

"But . . ."

"I whipped him, Father, with a switch. I whipped him good for hurting the young men. He ran off at first, but then he came back last night, like a little dog that wants to be friends."

"How did you cross the river?"

"I don't know what to say."

"Say the truth."

"I guess I do things girls are not supposed to do. People will not like me if they know. Ride Away doesn't like me to win a horse race against him. He doesn't like me to ride a horse he cannot ride."

"How did you cross the river, Horse Tender? No person could swim that. The best swimming horse might without a rider."

"Will you get angry with me if I say the truth?"

"No."

"I rode Smoke, Father."

After a long pause he said, "You must have horse medicine. It's very rare, even for a man."

"I think maybe I do."

Antelope Man thought about the matter. It was true that the rising river and the flooded property had caused the people to forget about the horse and girl being north of the river. But there was the young man's broken arm. Someone might say bad medicine was involved. He asked Horse Tender to stay out of camp and keep Smoke out of sight a few days until the river went down or until the camp moved. He went and brought her bow and arrows, then said he had better go back and bring her some fire. But she said that she could make fire. He had begun to believe that maybe she could do whatever she said she could.

Ride Away was among the older of those young men who were still in warrior training and he, together with two others of equal maturity, got the privilege of going on a revenge raid. A Crow band had lost three lives, that of warrior and an old woman and a small child, to Cheyenne raiders. The Crows brought the war pipe to High Owl, who quickly put together a group of ten mature warriors and three young men to aid their brother band. The revenge party stayed away two weeks in that land to the east, and the High Owl contingent returned with honor and a Cheyenne scalp.

The three young men had been used to stand guard as wolves, to gather firewood, to hold horses. None of the three had got to see an enemy Cheyenne.

At her horse-guarding chores, Horse Tender

found the opportunity as soon as possible to ask
Ride Away about his great adventure. He depre-
cated his part in it and at the same time obviously
felt proud. When he said that he had heard two
shots fired, she laughed.

"What's funny?" he asked.

"Nothing. Did you see the enemy camp?"

"No, but I knew it was just over the hill. What's
funny?"

"Nothing."

"Nothing? You don't take it seriously. We were
in enemy country. If the Cheyennes had caught me,
they sure would have killed me."

"I'm sorry. I'll take it seriously."

"It's easy to sit here safe and laugh, but out there
it was serious even if they wouldn't let me do much.
Besides, I didn't start bragging about it; you asked
me. Then you laugh."

"I'm sorry, Ride Away. I think you're a hero.
Let's forget it and go get in some practice with the
bow."

"Hero! Stop acting that way. You know I didn't
do anything."

"I'm sorry."

"You should be," he said. "Why did you laugh?
And if we practice with the bow, I don't want you
to act like you're teaching me something. I know as
much as you do."

"I'm sorry, Ride Away. Actually I admire you.
Really I do. That's not for fun or anything. It's
true."

"Well, all right." He rose from the spot of grass
where they sat, thought a minute, then said, "I admire you too." Perhaps he was about to say, "You
can ride and shoot," but thought better of it. He

said, "You're goodlooking and you're the only girl in the band who doesn't giggle."

"Thank you. Were you scared on the raid?"

"No, of course not. You do get more tense the closer you get to the enemy. Maybe I was scared a little bit. It makes you realize how great the warriors are; it's life or death for them, and they know what to do and everything."

They went to practice together with their bows. It was important to him because of the contests with the young men and boys shooting at a still mark or at a rolling hoop. He was winning many of the contests. For him, this was important, for it would bring him to the attention of the leaders of High Owl's band.

Though he had an excellent family background, Ride Away, like other young Crows, had to prove himself as an individual. He was the grandson of old One Good Eye, a medicine man who was a Tobacco Planter, a Keeper of the Seeds; however, Ride Away could never amount to anything more than what he showed personally to his fellow tribesmen.

Sometimes Horse Tender said such as this to him: "It's not the distance; its the time the arrow is in flight. It's sixty steps to the first tree and that much again to the second tree, but the arrow slows down. It takes one heartbeat to the first trunk, but three from here to the second.

"So, with this wind, quartering from the left, aim one handspan to the left for the first trunk, but aim three for the second."

He pretended not to listen to her advice, but let her pick which of his arrows should be discarded, which straightened, which refeathered, and he won shooting contests. It was a delicate balance between the envy and admiration each held for the other and the pride he felt and the pride she felt with no kind of social justification.

Ride Away often felt uncomfortable in these days as he took part in the contests for the young men, for some of the participants were clearly not men, but boys. This was so in a meat-stealing game sponsored by the Big Dog Soldier Society. One morning at sunrise a leader of the society went around the camp paths calling out: "Meat thieves! Women, protect your food! Meat thieves all day until sundown! Word has come that hungry young warriors are on the prowl! Take warning! Cooked meat! Fresh meat! Dry meat! Watch your food! Meat thieves!"

Soon many of the women were scurrying around, taking into their tepees any large supplies of meat that were lying or hanging in an exposed spot. Most of them left a few strips hanging on their drying racks or a couple of chunks cooling in a kettle in the dooryard. Here and there an old woman perched herself on a small stack of firewood with a willow switch, looking all around at the trees and brush outside of camp, trying to seem like a determined defender.

Young males from the age of fifteen winters to those up in their twenties were obviously absent that morning. Everyone knew that they were somewhere out on the creek plastering themselves with mud for disguise and plotting strategy and bragging.

As the day wore on screams and laughter and loud scolding erupted sporadically as attempts were made on the camp. When a woman turned her back for a minute or dozed off, a lithe gray or brown form would dart from any shadow and make off with a piece of the meat she was supposed to be guarding. If a young thief were struck by a woman, he had to drop his prize. Cheers and loud teasing rose from all members of the camp, men, women, and children, sometimes for the meat owners, sometimes for the thieves.

About an hour before sunset, a commotion started at one end of camp on account of two stealing attempts. At the same time Horse Tender ran through the trees outside the other end of camp. She whispered loudly into a patch of sumac.

"Ride Away! Are you in there?"

"Get away! Can't you see I'm hiding?"

"Listen quick. A whole deer is hanging in the tree beside High Owl's lodge. He killed it yesterday. Now he's gone over to talk to Rainy."

"What are you talking about?"

"If you hurry this minute you can get away with it. All three of his wives have run down there to find out about the laughing and shouting. You have to go right now."

"Horse Tender, you must be crazy."

"You're standing there losing the chance," she said. "And you look pretty silly with mud all over you."

"Will you get out of here?" he demanded.

She left him alone.

About sundown the young men went to a deep hole in the creek to bathe, then, together with a few members of the Big Dog Soldier Society, built up a fire just outside the village to cook a big feast of their pilfered food. The big feast was uncertain in both quality and quantity. Sometimes an old woman called out to them: "If you boys get hungry, you can come beg your mothers for something to eat." The older men teased both the younger men and the women.

The following day Horse Tender found Ride Away out where both their horse bands grazed together. She said, "Can I ask you about yesterday?"

"I'm not going to take part in that nonsense next year," he said.

"I want to ask you—why don't the young men get more meat? It looks plain that if they made enough noise on one side of camp, the women would relax their guard on the other side."

"If anyone is smart enough to do that, he's too old to play the game. You don't seem to realize it's a game."

"If you're going to play it at all, seems like you should do your best."

"You don't understand, Horse Tender. It's practice in hiding, slipping around, fooling people. Those things are important on the warpath."

"Then why didn't you take the deer?"

"Why? Why? He's the civil chief of the band! Don't you know they would find out who did it? A thing like that? It might be a secret at first, but the young men would talk and the Big Dogs would talk and finally everybody in camp would know who took the deer."

"Well, weren't High Owl's wives warned to watch their meat like all the others?"

"A whole deer! Horse Tender, you must be crazy!"

"Is there a rule you have to steal only small pieces? You and the others could have had a big feast and not get teased."

"You simply don't understand. You don't know how High Owl and the other chiefs think. You don't seem to respect them."

"I think it's you who don't respect them," she said. "If I were High Owl, I would be searching for bold young men who might lead the band twenty years from now when the present chiefs are old or gone. Yesterday, if I were High Owl, I would have hung a fresh-dressed deer in a tree by my lodge to find out if anyone could take it from under the eyes of three women who had been warned to watch it."

At this Ride Away became angry and would not speak to her until the middle of the afternoon, when she had broiled two fat ducks and came to beg him to eat with her.

"If you make any jokes about me acting hungry," he told her, "I'm going to hit you with a hot duck."

It was in the autumn before the horse Smoke would become a three-year-old. High Owl's band had camped well up on Thick Ash Tree Creek at a point where the timber clears and the draws that lead up away from the stream are choked with plum bushes. Frost came on the grass each dawn, and the plums had turned sugary with their tartness. Dried, the fruit was excellent to mix with pounded buffalo meat and bone marrow to make pemmican. Bears and coyotes competed for the sweet fruit.

The women went out picking daily, each bringing home all she could carry. At first they picked those nearest camp and easiest of access; then they began to scatter and go farther in search of richer harvests. Their diligence brought tragedy to one woman and her kin.

One afternoon two women came running into camp, crying and telling that they had heard the terrible screams of a woman, along with the growls and grunts of an angry bear. They led a dozen men up to the spot of the encounter. The plum thicket was torn up. They found the woman victim mortally wounded. She had been mauled, clawed, and bitten. Large bear tracks covered the ground in the thicket.

The woman died of blood loss while they were fashioning a litter of poles and a buffalo robe to carry her home. Her family wailed for her all night. In the morning they dressed her in her favorite dress, with beadwork on its front, and wrapped her neatly in a good robe. Inside the wrapping they put her plum-gathering bag, her root-digging stick, and her hide scraper. In a quiet place downstream they hoisted her to the crotch of a tree and tied her securely. There she would be out of the reach of prowling carnivore, and her spirit would be free to go on the wind.

The people were accustomed to violence and sometimes death.

About noon of that day Elk Head, who was currently chief of the Fox Society, led five heavily armed soldier warriors to clear the nearby area of bears. They took two trade guns as well as bows and freshly sharpened knives. They came back before evening with a huge bear skin and the bloody heart of the beast pinioned on a green stick.

The Fox Society soldier went through the camp to gather all the young men who were grown, but untried as warriors, to come to a sacred ceremony.

In the center of the village the Fox men built a fire and began to broil the bear's heart, which was as big as the two doubled fists of a man. The nine young men who had been gathered, including Ride Away, waited silently. All other business in camp had ceased. The people, including Horse Tender and the others of Antelope Man's lodge, stood back at a respectful distance to observe. They chatted, but did not laugh nor talk loudly.

When the meat was done, each Fox member sprinkled it with a bit of water to cool it. Then Elk Head took the heart and began to slice a portion for each of the young men, who were lined in a half circle facing him. Elk Head spoke something to each in a low voice.

"The bear is not afraid of any enemy."

The chatter among the watchers stopped. As the ceremony proceeded, not even a baby or a dog made a sound. They could hear part of what the society leader said.

"Eat this; fear will never keep you from being a good warrior."

"These are your comrades sharing this food; each will fight like a bear beside you."

"You will defend the Crow nation with your brave heart."

As the young men ate, the watchers felt deeply solemn. Here and there a woman, perhaps watching a son or younger brother, wept silently and could not have given a reason for the tears; it was a joining of unnamed joy and sorrow.

Horse Tender's bow did not have the range or force to kill big game at a distance. She spent hours stalking deer and elk, with no success, for such animals became skittish near an Indian camp and she did not want to wound one and let it get away. The hunting of buffalo was supervised by one of the soldier societies, and they frowned upon solitary hunters of this valuable game.

Together with Ride Away, she worked out a way to kill antelope on the open rolling prairie far from any timber. At first they only raced their horses against the fast animals; then they found that they could actually exhaust the fleet game, if there were not too many gullies or prairie dog holes in the area.

Upon finding a small band, they would separate to opposite sides, one riding almost out of sight in the distance, as far away as a horse can run at full speed. The one nearby would flush the game and, when the animals scattered, would follow the one or two that were going in the right direction, pressing as fast as possible. Then the second chaser would take over, allowing the antelope no rest. This rider's job was to turn the game in a large circle back to where the first rider rested. Then the first rider became the third chaser and, after wearing down a horse for the second time, might find it necessary to jump off and run afoot after the antelope with bow and arrow at the ready. If the plan had worked to this point, the exhausted game could be easily dispatched.

With their horse-herding chores, they seldom got more than two or three antelope a week. Some of the meat they cooked on the prairie; most of it they packed home to their families, along with the skins.

Smoke was the best mount for both speed and stamina in either of the two herds. He would not let Ride Away get on him. Ride Away argued with Horse Tender about it and complained, "I let you ride any of my horses you want to."

"Well, you can ride any of mine," she said.

"You know he's an outlaw. If you would make him, he would let me."

"You're too heavy."

"Heavy? That horse could carry three men like me. It's past time for him to be castrated. When Antelope Man castrates him, then he'll calm down."

Horse Tender immediately went to work on her adopted father, at every opportunity when they could talk alone, begging him not to have Smoke castrated. He was already tame. It wasn't fair. It was cruel to do a horse like that. She even said she would give Smoke a good whipping with a switch and make him let Antelope Man ride.

He had been counting on a good hunting horse and war-horse and had believed that Smoke would be trainable, docile, when he was made into a gelding. He had been putting off the castration; these days his old foot wound was giving him a lot of trouble. He could pay one robe sometime when the men were working horses, and have the job done; but if the young stallion objected, there might be more broken bones and fees to pay medicine men. He decided to let Horse Tender have her way.

Antelope Man joked a little with his friends about it, saying, "If one of your mares comes up with a first-class black foal, you can pay me something for a stud fee."

They would answer, "Gave up on that outlaw, did you?"

"I don't believe a good stud should be broke to work," Antelope Man would say.

6. Ride Away

It had become obvious to the two of them that Ride Away was stronger, but Horse Tender was quicker. Their friendship was good; though they argued frequently, they made up equally often. They were not like two boys, nor two girls, nor a brother and sister. Neither could have explained their relationship; perhaps it was unique. She protected her right to be his equal, and he protected his right to be hers.

She was older than some girls in the band who were already purchased wives. Most of the young men Ride Away's age had not yet married, since they needed war honors and also wealth to pay for a bride and to establish a lodge; only some of the men from the wealthiest families could afford to get married young.

In addition to helping each other herd horses and hunting together, they played almost like children. If she found him asleep, she would put a grasshopper down his neck; then when he awoke she would say, "Do you have fleas? I saw a big flea go down your neck." Getting even, he would put a frog down her dress and tell her it was a snake.

They found water holes far enough from camp

that they could swim in private. He took off all his clothes except a breechclout; she took off only her moccasins.

One late afternoon they had gone to a deep swimming hole that ran in a long curve under the shade of giant cottonwoods. They had gotten small, stickerlike seeds sometimes called beggar's-lice in their clothes. At the water's edge they splashed water on each other and threw mud. Ride Away took his clothes out in the water to wash them. Horse Tender swam farther upstream and took off her dress to get the beggar's-lice out.

He swam underwater toward her and rose up nearby. With a small gasp she stood up in the chest-deep water. They looked at each other without speaking. Her naked breasts were well developed.

It could hardly have been an accidental confrontation between two innocents. Perhaps one of them deliberately intended to seduce the other. More likely both of them had unconsciously arranged the matter.

It was nearly dark, time when they ordinarily would have caught their mounts and galloped back toward camp. They said nothing about it, nor did they play like children. Their desires seemed to make a bond that did not need to be discussed. Of the two robes that they used folded for saddles, they made a bed on the grass not far from the water. Their wet clothes they put to dry on a bush.

Ride Away got up without waking her at the first hint of dawn, for he had to deliver a certain horse to his father in camp. He returned in midmorning. She had dressed and moved the robes near a bank that hung over the creek. She lay smiling as he approached.

"You're a brute," she said.

"No I'm not."

"Yes you are. You made me bleed last night."

"I'm sorry."

"You should be. You're an old mean buffalo bull."

"I'm sorry."

"Did you bleed?"

"No, boys don't bleed."

"Let me see."

"Horse Tender! You're the most shameless woman that ever lived."

"Well, if you're really sorry why don't you come here and hug me."

He knelt down and started to put his arms around her. She put her hands on his waist and rolled over and pushed; he lost his balance and fell sprawling into the water below the bank. She looked over and asked, "Did you fall?" Floundering and spluttering, he said something like, "Wait till I get my hands on you!"

She ran and he chased her, through the trees, sometimes splashing across a shallow part of the creek. He yelled as if angry and she screamed appropriately when he came near. When she finally allowed him to catch her, they were too breathless to get revenge or to resist. They rested, holding hands, and realized that they both were famished and needed to plan to make some food.

After that, they spent one or two nights a week away from camp, making love, sporting, playing.

The Absarokas had known as neighbors and allies the Kiowa tribe only a generation earlier. The Kiowas had moved far south down the plains, but were still thought of as close friends. There had been some intermarriage between the groups. Those in the Crow nation who had some Kiowa blood often said. "If they don't visit us this year, we should go visit them next year."

Finally, as the horses were getting fat on new spring grass, members from several bands agreed to make the trek south, which would take a month each way. Some thirty men and an equal number of women would go. They would do a little trading, but mostly visiting.

Antelope Man, who had lived a year with a Kiowa family as a boy, was having trouble with his foot, but, perhaps believing it would be his last chance to make the trip, decided to go. He would take Birdy with him. As the plans were being made, Horse Tender got him to come outside of camp for a private talk.

"What's this big talk?" he asked. "I may as well say now that you can't go. I depend on you to do things here."

"No, Father, it's about trees they have away down in the south country."

"Trees? What's this?"

"Somewhere down there grows a tree they call *bois d'arc*. It's the same that Chicago said they call Osage orange. I believe it's the greatest bow wood in the world, along with one other. It has a kind of snap to it."

"But why do you say this? We are only going on a visit."

"Please don't say no, Father, until you let me explain. I need a piece of *bois d'arc* or else a bow made of it."

"How do you know about this wood?"

"Two Fox Society men have bows of it. When the young men shot for distance, one of them used

one of those bows, and he always won. A long time
ago, before I found you for my father, there was an
Atsina man and two Blackfoot men; they had bows
of it, which they had traded from the Mandans.
You remember that bunch of Shoshones last year.
The old man with gray hair, he had a bow of it, but
I don't know how he got it, but I think he's kin to
the Comanches, who also live down there south
with the Kiowas where the tree grows. The way
they cut the bow, they leave some heartwood and
some sapwood, so that they make it brittle and also
strong."

He said, "I don't believe you ever forget a thing
you see or hear. What's so different about his *bois
d'arc* tree?"

"It's the snap and the strength together. I believe
there are two great bow woods. There is a foreign
tribe called *English* and they have a tree they call
yew. Chicago says that all the greatest bowmen
who ever lived on earth have shot *yew* or *bois
d'arc.*"

Antelope Man was standing with his hands
clasped behind him, his shoulders slumped. "Don't
you like the bow I gave you?"

"Yes, I love it. It shoots true."

"Do you have any idea, daughter, how much I
put up to make the price of that sheep's horn
bow?"

"Yes, I knew from the first. Someone who was
an artist must have spent a whole winter working
on it. It's a bow that cost too much and was made
for the youngest pet wife of a wealthy chief. It's a
woman's bow."

"You're a woman. You could not pull a man's
bow."

"Well, what I need, Father, is a strong man's

bow; then I can finish scraping it to give it balance and make it true and make it right for me. It must have stock on it for me to cut away carefully. Then I could try it and scrape, try it and scrape. Although I love the first bow you gave me, you could trade it for such a bow down south, and because the special trees grow there, maybe you can get some extra boot for presents to give the women of your lodge."

He still seemed reluctant. "You kill antelope with your bow."

"Father, we chase them down. I have to get close."

"What? No one can chase down an antelope!"

"Well, yes, Father. I have to get real close to pierce their heart. We chase them on horseback and afoot. They get exhausted, and we can get them for food. Father, I have never got an elk or a grown buffalo and only one white-tailed deer."

"Who's we?" he asked.

"Ride Away. He's the grandson of One Good Eye and a nice young man."

He said, "Now, Horse Tender, I want you to be careful. That young man is of a good family, but they should all be suspected. They will take advantage of you. You see, well, you don't know how pretty you are. A young man thinks of only one thing. Well . . . he thinks about your body, daughter. He can't help it. He thinks about between your legs and his mind keeps coming back to it and he dwells on it. You have to be on guard. You can chase antelopes with him, but don't be alone with him. Do you understand what I mean? *Magahawathus!* Above on high! You should have a mother to tell you!"

"Yes, Father, it's all right. I understand."

"Well, be on guard."

"Yes, Father. Then can I have the bow? Will you please get it for me? Please?"

"What can I do?" he said. "I'll do my best. What am I going to do with you? Horse Tender, you are riding my stud Smoke, which cannot be ridden, and chasing down antelope, which are faster than jackrabbits, and shooting ducks out of the air! What am I going to do with you?"

"Father, it's all right. I'm the luckiest girl in the world to get you for a father, because you're understanding. You will get me the bow?"

"Yes, I'll get it."

"Do you leave tomorrow?"

"Yes."

"The stars will be different down there. The star that does not move, you will be able to see it drop lower. Since you told me about stars, I have been studying them. When you come home, you can tell me how the skies look down south."

"I'll study them and tell you," he said.

"They say down there the southern sky has a pattern shaped like a scorpion, with a red star for a head. He crawls up in the southeast, then over and down in the southwest."

"I'll look for it and tell you."

"Father?"

"Yes."

"Tomorrow when you go, other people will be around. Can I say good-by to you now?"

He spread his arms out and they embraced. She said, "Be careful and don't get hurt in that strange country. Come home safe to us."

That evening she brought into camp the two rid-

ing horses and two pack horses that Antelope Man
and Birdy would take. The next morning all was a
bustle around the tepee as the two prepared to
leave. Antelope Man asked the women of his lodge
to be quiet, for he had a few words to say. The limp
that had afflicted him recently had disappeared,
perhaps because of the excitement of the coming
journey.

"Pay a little attention," he said. "I have decided
to take Horse Tender's bow. She does not need
such a valuable bow, and maybe I can trade it off
down south.

"Now I want things to go in an orderly way here
while I'm gone. No bickering. My first wife See
Dead Bull is in charge. I want her to keep a proper
and decent lodge, for we are a family with a good
reputation. My shield and spear and larger medicine bag I leave with her; no one else should touch
them.

"Her honored mother lives with us and is to be
shown respect. My beloved aunt, Pea Finder, is
also to be shown respect.

"I leave my bow and quiver and arrows with
Horse Tender. I order her to bring in at least one
mess of fresh game each week, more if possible. I
want everyone to act right the way I tell you. If I
find out different when I get back, I'll get angry.
And you know how I am when I get angry."

"Ask your husband," Broken Ice said, "if that
Slave Girl is to be allowed to stay out at night
whenever she pleases. It's shameful."

"As for Horse Tender," he said, "she knows
how to hunt and care for my horses the way I
taught her. If she decides to stay away at night, it is
up to her. If my first wife asks for a horse to drag

wood or for any other purpose, I order Horse Tender to bring the horse. If the camp moves, See Dead Bull is in charge; Horse Tender shall take care of my herd. All should obey the chief and do right."

"Ask your husband," said Broken Ice, "if that Slave Girl is supposed to do any work around here like all the rest of us do."

"Tell your mother," he said, "that this is my last word. I'm trying to be clear. I don't say anyone can lie around while others work. I am the man of this lodge and you better believe it. If I turn my back a few days, everyone can act right. I want no cross words, no backbiting, no bickering."

Other travelers were already in their saddles. He briefly caressed See Dead Bull and Pea Finder. Broken Ice seemed well satisfied that her son-in-law could not touch her. Birdy hugged everyone. They headed south, leading the two pack horses.

In those days if Horse Tender spent the night in camp, she would go early after water, bringing all she could carry in bags and an iron kettle. Otherwise Pea Finder would probably be assigned the task and would labor half a day at it. Horse Tender spent much time away from camp in order to avoid any arguments—also to be with Ride Away, to test out the strong bow that Antelope Man had left with her, and to make sure the horse herd was well tended.

Though they played and teased, Ride Away and Horse Tender often held hands as they sat together or walked together along the creek. They knew where to meet, either by spoken agreement or considered guess, and when they saw each other com-

ing, they would run in order to meet sooner. Their
greeting might be tender or foolish, such as: "I'm
sorry to tell you; all your horses died last night."
"What?" "Yes, a prairie dog scared them, and they
stampeded over a cliff."

They gave up chasing antelope in favor of stalking game. With the new bow she could shoot twice
as far, though she was not satisfied with the accuracy. Ride Away teased her, saying that the bow
was accurate enough, but too strong for her.

Early one morning during the first moon after
Antelope Man and Birdy left, she killed an elk, a
fat young cow. It was with great pride that she
packed in the skin and all the meat except one side
of ribs. Pea Finder exclaimed over the meat. The
other two women said nothing, but they immediately set to work taking care of the meat and
flashing the hide.

If Horse Tender and Ride Away only held hands
or made love or played or kept busy hunting, they
got along well; but in those quiet times when they
rested and talked, they always came to an argument. One day as they sat on a bleached log, he
said in great seriousness: "I think I know what's
important. You get a lot of ideas while you're
growing up, but it's simpler than all those and it's
more than those, too. It's just medicine and
bravery. That's all. That covers it all. If you get in
tune with Earth and all the Powers. Then you are
not afraid to die or afraid to get hurt. What else is
there? Maybe I would say you should also tell the
truth. It's important in council to say what you
know and think and want. It all boils down to
those: medicine and bravery and telling the truth in
council."

"How about telling the truth outside of council?" she asked.

"Horse Tender, I'm serious. I'm not joking. Everyone knows that you should treat your family fair, and people like that."

She withdrew her hand from his and cupped her hands under her chin. "What do they say in sweat lodges?"

"What?"

"In sweat lodges. The men, what do they talk about?"

"Horse Tender, what's the matter with you? I can't tell you secrets about other men's medicine. Anyway, a woman doesn't need to know."

"I don't think lovers should have secrets from each other."

"What does being lovers have to do with it?"

"You don't even act like a friend."

"Let's forget it," he said, "and go swimming."

"I don't want to go swimming with you. I don't even like you."

He began to try to mollify her and swore that he had no secrets from her, except in a few instances where certain men had taboos against revealing their medicine to a woman. He spoke of the sacred power called *ma-ash-pay,* or medicine, how every natural thing has a life in its own world and may take pity on a human person and give them luck and power. It might be a small stone or an animal or bird or anything.

"Could thunder be medicine?"

He laughed. "That's like asking if the sun could be medicine."

"Well, could it?"

"It's too powerful for personal medicine. A person who got thunder for personal medicine would be too proud to live and would be dangerous to himself even."

Ride Away at this time felt strongly the influence of the great warrior heroes of the past. He had as yet received no strong medicine, but hoped soon to get some through a vision or else as a gift from his grandfather. He expounded to Horse Tender the advantages of living to an old age and the advantages of dying young in battle; the latter course seemed better to him. He reiterated his opinion that running and riding and hiding and shooting and hunting were lesser abilities, that what mattered most was medicine and bravery.

"Wouldn't it be too bad," she said, "if a brave man was killed by a coward who was a better marksman?"

He glared at her.

"Well, wouldn't it?"

"Horse Tender, I've been talking seriously to you because you asked me to, and now you take it lightly and make fun of me."

"I only asked a question."

"You asked because sometimes you happen to shoot straighter than I do. You don't want to understand what I mean about bravery."

"I'm sorry, Ride Away. I'll listen. Tell me how you felt when you ate the slice of bear's heart."

"So you can make a joke?"

"No, I'm sorry. Really, tell me. Did you notice how quiet the whole camp got? And it seemed so solemn."

"All right, I'll tell you. When I ate the meat I felt it in my blood. I now *know* that I will never run in the face of an enemy. All I need is the chance to show bravery. And maybe medicine to protect me and give luck, though I don't care if I die young. I could feel it all through me."

He looked to see whether she would laugh or say something to tease, but she did not.

Two days later they had another argument. They had moved their horse herds around to another side of the village and into a valley where the grass seed stood thick, cured golden tan. They showed the horses a water hole, then threw them out on the fresh pasture and dismounted under some elm trees. Horse Tender said angrily to him, "Why did you come down that slope like that? You hurt your horse!"

"What do you mean? What slope?"

"You know what I mean! Coming off that high bench over there. You whipped him all the way in a dead run. Don't you understand that hurts a horse's shoulders?"

"You're serious, aren't you. You don't like to be outridden by anybody."

"Can't you understand? Look at your horse! He's still trembling. You're going to make a cripple out of him."

"I don't think I ride any more wild than you do."

"It wasn't a race! You might at least have let him pick his way. Can't you tell by the way a horse steps that it hurts his shoulders to run down a steep hill?"

"Horse Tender, forget it. Let's don't talk about it."

"I don't want to forget it. You boys and men talk about medicine and how some animal will become your friend and give you magic power. And you can't even feel a horse's shoulders hurting when you're sitting on top of him!"

"Listen, girl, I don't need you to tell me about horses. What made you so wise?"

"You don't have to be wise to know better than that."

"Well, I don't want your advice."

"Well, you won't get it anymore. You can stay away from me. I hope I never see you again."

"That's all right with me," he said.

They did not speak to each other for a week. Then they chanced to go swimming at the distant water hole at the same time. They came out holding hands. Later she said, "I'm sorry I talked so smart and wise," and he said, "I'm sorry too; I know better than to run a horse downhill." She said, "It was only that it hurt me for a while. I felt his shoulders hurting, you know? It went all through me. I could feel it in my blood."

Antelope Man came home from the south on a litter made of two long poles and a robe called *canvas*, this carried by four horsemen or by four men afoot. Antelope Man had been kicked by a Comanche pack mule into a pile of prickly pears. His old foot wound had seemed all right, but now the same leg was swelled up twice as big as normal from the many stickers. He could not walk and could hardly stand. Birdy had dressed the leg with cornmeal poultice and with crushed-leaf poultice the best she could.

The women installed him in a bed of grass and robes under the arbor beside the tepee. He was not in much pain, but was full of talk about what they had seen on the journey. The Kiowas and their allies were generous people. He would like to move down there, he said, except that it was too hot. He distributed to Broken Ice, See Dead Bull, and Pea Finder a quantity of trade beads of different colors, also a small bag of brass tacks for decorating wooden handles.

He had traded off Horse Tender's horn bow and gave her instead a large, crude wooden bow. It had belonged to a chief who had grown too old for the warpath and had determined to make a great bow, but had become feeble before he could finish it.

As Horse Tender examined it in the sunlight, Pea Finder said, "I'm sorry about your bow."

She said, "No, see! This is it! It's *bois d'arc.*"

"Well, I'm sorry about your beautiful bow."

"No, look! It's cured perfectly. Not a crack. It's great."

Pea Finder said, "It looks ugly. Just hacked out."

"We'll fix that," she said.

Later when she got a chance she hugged Antelope Man and he asked, "Is that what you meant?" and she said, "Yes, Father, that's exactly what I meant."

She began to shoot with the bow and scrape on it with a keen whetted knife.

Later in the autumn, after the first snow fell, the band made winter camp on *Ets-pot-agie,* or Mountain Sheep River, or as the first traders called it *Gros Cornu.* At the mouth of this stream, where it ran into the Elk, white persons had built a trading post of log houses and a high picket fence, but it was now abandoned and burned down. After discussing the matter with Chicago, Horse Tender rode downstream to the old site. She stirred with a digging stick in a place where they had thrown away worthless things and scraps and such. Those people had small containers made of something called *glass* which they broke often. She picked up a bag full of the broken material, some curved, some flat.

The *glass* was excellent for scraping. If its edge became dull, it had only to be broken again to produce new sharp edges. During the coldest spells that winter, when no one went out into the weather unless it was necessary, Horse Tender spent long hours scraping the *bois d'arc,* drawing from the hard wood handfuls of cuttings as fluffy as rabbit fur. She took the bow out to try it after each session of work on it.

When she had smoothed it and tapered it and balanced it to suit herself, she took an old fire-hardened chokecherry arrow and rubbed the bow hard all over to close the pores of the wood so that it would not absorb moisture readily.

That winter, in addition to the game she had been accustomed to kill, Horse Tender packed in the meat and skins of three elk and two buffalos. Also she got four wolf skins; Chicago would trade Antelope Man plenty of tobacco and sugar for those.

7. A Lonely Meal

She rode the stallion Smoke anywhere she wished without apology or explanation. Most of the band must have thought that the outlaw horse had run away and that this was another, for they made no issue of the matter. Nor did most of the band members think odd the fact that though Antelope Man was usually laid up with his bad leg, his lodge always had plenty of meat.

Yet the underground rumors about her persisted —among the inconsequential, the children, the *berdaches*, the very old. They said that she prayed to Thunder. Perhaps exaggerating, they said that with a magic bow she had fashioned she could shoot as far as any man.

High Owl's band had moved that spring to *Etspot-agie cate*, or Little Mountain Sheep River, called by the early white traders *Petite Cornu*. As early summer came on wild roses bloomed in the area; their vines hung down the slopes and banks along the stream, and their tender pink flowers made the air sweet.

The little river was clear and icy cold. It was flanked on both sides with rolling sagebrush hills, but the broad bottom of the valley was fertile and lush with glades of box elder and cottonwood. The winding valley seemed also fertile to the attraction between young men and women, for they flirted and courted profusely up and down the banks of the river; seven couples of the band had married that spring and set up new lodges.

One day Horse Tender and Ride Away had ridden far upstream. She had been moody, and he had asked her several times, "What's the matter?"

As they sat on a patch of green grass in the shade she said, "Ride Away, I want to be courted."

"Well," he said, "we don't need to go back to the village. I'll court you all night tonight."

"That's not what I mean."

"The moon will be out tonight. We can swim and eat and make love."

"Nice girls don't stay out alone with men when they're not married to them."

He started several times to say something, then said, "We're different. Let the others do what the old men and women in proper families say. Courting and permission and buying a wife is a bunch of nonsense."

"The other girls don't think it is. I see them making eyes at you and walking on purpose so their hips sway."

"I don't even look at them."

"Yes, you do. I saw you look at that daughter from Rainy's lodge."

"Horse Tender, I have to look somewhere. Do you expect me to go around with my eyes closed?"

"I want to be courted," she said.

He became angry. "You're the most unreasonable person I ever saw! You wouldn't even stand still long enough for a man to court you."

An edge came into her voice. "What is that supposed to mean?"

"Well, why don't you go to your lodge and twice a day carry water, and I will stand near the path and we will smile at each other. When you go to carry wood, I will come near where you are working with other women, and we will make eyes at each other. I will carve me a little flute, and while you are scraping hides at your lodge I will hide back in the brush and tootle love music, and old See Dead Bull will probably throw rocks at me."

She said quickly, "Don't you call my mother old."

He shouted, "What do you expect me to do?"

"I could get other men to court me," she said. "You might at least give me a present some time. When Antelope Man goes on a journey he brings back a gift of jewelry for his wives."

"I don't have any jewelry. Where would I get jewelry? And don't tell me you could get other men! I could court other girls. Plenty of them."

"I hope you do," she said, "because I don't want to ever see you again."

"That's fine with me," he said.

A week later when High Owl's band moved southwest toward the Bighorn Mountains the two of them cooperated in driving the horse bands, but said no kind words to each other.

Chicago rode toward where Horse Tender sat near a small cook fire, a long hour's ride from the village. He yelled ahead to her, "Ho! Ho! There you are," making sure that he did not seem to sneak up. She was not hidden, but had built her fire on a broad gravel bed by a dry wash.

"So this is whereabouts you hide yourself," he said, dismounting.

She smiled. "I hide where the hunting is good, or where my horse herd goes."

"You ain't been home in two, three days."

"Is anything interesting happening in camp?"

"Well, maybe Antelope Man's lodge could use some meat."

"I don't think so. I packed in three deer last week. They probably still give meat away."

She had a piece of dark meat larger than a man's fist pinned on a sharpened stick, the other end of the stick set firmly in the gravel. From the hot meat had been cut slices as the outside became cooked.

"Damn my rusty soul," he said, as if forcing himself to sound friendly. "Looks like I got here just in time for lunch." Strangely, whenever his eyes happened to fix on the chunk of cooking meat, he moved them away as if it were improper to look at it.

She said, "Sorry I didn't cook you anything."

"You going to eat the rest of that?"

"Yes." She laughed at him and said, "If you're really hungry I have a rabbit I got this morning and dressed and wrapped in wet grass to keep it cool. In my pack I have some suet to slice thin over the rabbit while he broils. Even a sprinkle of salt. Do you want it? It won't take long."

He was cutting from a plug of tobacco and putting it in his mouth with his knife blade. "I don't reckon so. Fact is, I come to talk to you, Little Gal."

"I didn't think you were hungry in the first place."

"How come you stay out alone like this?"

She did not answer.

"I know more than you think I do, Little Gal. I got the damndest strange story to tell you; I was to tell it some places they'd call me a big liar." She laughed a little and put her hands on her hips as he went on.

"Four of the Fox Society boys made up to go on yonder mountains to see if any friends or enemies was camped in the valley on the other side. It's a hard day's ride one way. I went with them. I ain't as young as I once was, but I figured if we found any Crows I'd let them know what trade goods I got.

"We didn't see nothing, but it was on the way back yesterday we run into this strange mystery. We come down across the head of Little Snake Creek. There's a big plum patch up there with plums starting to drop. You know whereabouts that is?"

She was holding the meat by sticking it with a small knife while she sliced with a larger. "It's out there," she said vaguely.

"In this opening in the patch we found the biggest, grayest he-grizzly bear I ever seen."

"Did you run?"

"No, this old critter was dead. But he wasn't even stiff yet."

She laughed. "I guess he ate too many sour plums and died of a bellyache."

"He died of a bellyache all right enough, and a chestache. Looked like he'd got one arrow, and the shaft pulled out, but he'd been stabbed about seven times in the chest and belly, and arms slashed like he was fighting a knife. He died hard."

She said nothing.

"I reckon you know what else we seen about that bear's chest. The four Fox Society members were too nervous even to take the hide for a rug or the claws for a necklace. Damn claws big as your finger. You want me to say what it was about the critter's chest?"

"I guess it was for that silly ceremony where boys eat a piece of the heart and get brave."

"I don't guess it was and you don't neither."

"Does all this bother you so much, Chicago?"

"Yes, Little Gal! Damnit yes! Going around doing like that! Damn yes! Fighting and risking that way for something that wasn't even needful in the first place. Are you a woman or what?"

"I'm a human being."

"What kind of human being goes around stabbing bears? Four times as big as they are!"

"Chicago, does all this really bother you so much?"

"Damn, hell yes! I tell you yes, it does! You got friends! You ain't lacking in people behind you! Quit pushing yourself and fighting yourself! I seen that bear's big arms! He was fighting a knife! Quit it, I tell you!"

She sliced a thin piece from the chunk of meat and stuffed it in her mouth. She said, "Bear people must give their blood and flesh to human people when the right time comes."

"Now, Little Gal, there is nothing magic about a bear's heart. You know this well as I do. In the ceremony for the boys, it's for their minds. It's for their feelings and their minds. Ain't nothing magic there. They will remember it in their minds all their lives."

She said, "Well, will you think about this? What about women? They are afraid; I'm scared of grizzly bears myself. What about their minds? They are scared of all the enemies around us, the tribes and other danger. What about their minds? See Dead Bull saw Elk River, *La Roche Jaune,* full of ice chunks, take her little boy and freeze him and batter him and drown him. You wonder why she's cruel? What about her mind?"

He paced back and forth, seemingly more agitated than she. "No, Little Gal, you don't understand. I ain't saying what I mean. The boys do it together. The meat is handed down by an older man, and the boys eat it together. After that, they trust each other all their lives. You got to trust them that's with you when you go to war."

She did not answer, but sliced another thin slice of hot meat and stuck it in her mouth.

He said passionately, "Is it bitter?"

In a moment she said, "It's kind of tough. Please don't be angry with me, Chicago."

"Who's angry? We're alike, you and me. But I've learned some things you ain't learned yet. We're outcasts. Look at me. I'm wanted in Missouri and Illinois too. They want to string me up with a rope on my neck and choke me to death. The Chippaways wants me and the Dakotas too; that's some trick to get both them bunches to want you at once. They want to shoot me and take my hair. Some other Injun people wants me the same way.

"But you know, Little Gal, my Crow people here want me. I got a sweet little wife and two kids. They don't care if I'm ugly or poor or ordinary. My friends here don't expect me to be a great, brave warrior. They like me anyway. What can a body ask for more than a family and friends? I found my place. You got friends here too, Little Gal."

She was eating the last of the hot meat, licking her fingers. Then she spoke softly and kindly. "I know it. I have Antelope Man and you and Birdy and Pea Finder and maybe others. I'm not an outcast. Please don't be angry and don't be worried. It will be all right."

"Don't be worried? What kind of words is that? You are headed for trouble. Listen to me! It's trouble soon and it's trouble down the road. There ain't no way you can win. Don't you see what I mean?"

"Win what?"

"Damnation!" he said. "What is anybody trying to do? A chief or a slave or the big King of England? Ain't none of us got but one life on this earth. I'm trying to tell you about trouble in the long run."

"Are you sure?" she asked. "Maybe we are not alike. Anyway, what's wrong with trouble?"

8. Year of the War Club Hunt

It did not seem surprising that *Maga-hawathus* had located his best people in the center of his best land. He had given the land to them and given them, along with the buffalo and fleet antelope and sagebrush and prairie rose, to the land.

It stretched north far beyond Big River, to Gun River and Bear River, and even farther into what some called the icy place of the Redcoats. From up there came the various divisions of the Blackfeet, the Blood and Piegan and main Blackfoot, pressing south past the Bearpaw Mountains into Crow country, raiding down past the Musselshell and the Crazy Mountains. West the land stretched into the snowcapped Beartooth and Absaroka ranges; south, past the Shoshonis and Cheyennes, past Wind River, as far as anyone might want to go into a land that is too warm. East it stretched to the Black Hills, which the Lakota, or Teton Sioux, were trying to invade and claim; also to the Mandans, who farmed along Big River, along with the Hidatsa, those close cousins of the Crow.

In this broad country *Maga-hawathus* put bountiful game and many edible roots and fruits. He put green valleys and streams of cold water. He also put, with his helpers, badlands, eroded soil and barren outcrops of rocks, rattlesnakes, prickly-pear cactus, and blizzards in winter so fierce that any creature caught unprotected on the plain would turn to ice. Above all, the Creator put space, distance, the big sky, so that a Crow Indian might look at the solitude and be awed, knowing the vast sweetness and bitterness at once in this best land where he belonged.

The heartland of Crow country was the valley of the Yellowstone, which Chicago, with a laugh, called Rocky John. Its rich tributaries included a number that came up from the south: the Powder, Tongue, Rosebud, Bighorn, Stinking Water, Arrow Creek, and others. All watered great herds of elk, deer, buffalo, antelope. It was no wonder that other peoples felt envious.

The most dangerous invaders were the Sioux. The Crow bands got warning information from many sources: from slaves taken or escaped, from wandering white traders like Chicago, from sporadic visits to trading forts on Big River, from pilgrimages such as that to visit the Kiowas, from a dozen neighboring peoples who were neutral at times, if not allies. The warnings had gradually taken an ominous turn; among the western Sioux had risen a war chief named Streaked Hair, who swore that the westward advance of his people would not be blocked. Some said he had reasons for vengeance against the Crow, but all sources agreed that he wanted not merely a few scalps, but the extinction of the Crow Nation. High Owl's council questioned Chicago at length about the immediate danger; he would only assert that his own heart and blood were pure Crow, like his wife and children, that he had traded neither gun nor powder nor lead to the Sioux for ten years, that he had long ago heard Sioux braggarts and was not afraid, that he would stand alongside Crow warriors any day. The council decreed that Streaked Hair should not be noticed any more than any other enemy, but that the Fox Warrior Society should regularly station wolves on high ground outside their camp to prevent surprises of the band.

That autumn High Owl's people went into the valley of Powder River for a fall meat and robe hunt. They moved cautiously, not to scare the buffalo, for they had not been lucky enough to find any sizable herd for several moons. The broad, shallow river was so muddy that even the horses did not like to drink it; the fine sand along its banks stirred into the air with the wind and left a film of dust on the autumn foliage. War Club Society scouts reported a good herd nearby, and High Owl's band made a quiet camp, holding their horse herds downstream behind them.

The War Club Soldier Society had been given for this occasion complete authority to scout and hold the buffalo and direct the hunt for the good of all. They called out the hunters and assembled them in a long scattered line just below the crest of a ridge.

They could see the muddy Powder off to their right.

Horse Tender rode Smoke up to a gap in the hunters' line. The society leader galloped toward her, his lumpwood club raised as a symbol of his authority. He said distinctly, without making much noise: "Go back with the women!"

"I hunt for the lodge of Antelope Man," she said.

"Go back with the women! Sharpen your butcher knives and hold your pack horses ready!"

"But I hunt for Antelope Man. A lodge of six people."

"Go back with the women! You hear me! I've told you three times."

Horse Tender pushed her quiver around to the front. "See the mark. One red line across one feather. It's Antelope Man's mark. I take his place."

He was a large man and certain that he was right. He sat his nervous horse with assurance. "Go back with the women! I have told you four times. That's enough! Now I call witnesses."

"What will we do for meat?"

He made sweeping motions with the warclub toward some members of the society who were within sight. Five of them reined toward him in a lope. She began saying, hurriedly: "I will ride just like the men. I will not scare anyone else's target. I will obey the instructions of the War Club men." But he was not listening.

When the five pulled up he said intensely, but not loudly: "This is not sport! This is not single hunting! This is food, dried meat, for ninety-four lodges for a winter! This is food or starvation! I have told this person four times to go back with the women! I should only tell her once! This is no time for special cases! We are about to begin the hunt!

"Now, you two men fit an arrow to your bow! You three raise your whips!"

He lowered his war club and raised a quirt with a long ash handle. "We are going to kill your horse! We are going to whip you till you are bloody all over! We are going to break your weapons to splinters! For the one time before witnesses: Go back with the women!"

She wheeled Smoke and kicked him toward the river, which she crossed, splashing. They did not follow. The society was turning loose the hunters.

Soon the earth shook with the rumble of hoofs. The buffalo could run in their bouncing, rolling gait as well as all but the fastest horses, but when the herd leaders tried to break out of the valley they found themselves turned back by whooping Indians, who had been stationed at strategic points.

The rolling hills, covered with sagebrush and bunch grass, now became spotted with the dark-brown hulks of downed buffaloes, arrows in them, their noses pouring blood. The slaughter ranged for miles up the valley. Society members tried to keep them from the river, allowing only the fastest, most desperate to cross over.

Horse Tender made her own private hunt over on the left side of the valley that day, without the aid of the War Club Soldier Society. Though the day was mild, she dripped with dusty sweat when she rode about noon back to where the women were butchering. She waved the women of Antelope Man's lodge across the river and guided them to a buffalo cow, downed on a grassy slope. As they dismounted from the pack horses, old Broken Ice said to her eldest daughter. "I hope you tell that husband of yours that I don't like this at all. If he wasn't always sick with a bad foot or a bad leg, we might have plenty of meat like other lodges."

Horse Tender, astride Smoke, her quiver empty, was obviously angry. She screamed, "Tell that mother of yours she should have more respect for the man of her lodge! Who is she! Let her be thankful for a good home!"

The old woman said deliberately, "I am a respectable Crow woman and a tepee cutter. I don't have to put up with insults from a slave. Why should I have to beg meat this winter?"

"If you will quit whining," Horse Tender said, "and get to work, you won't have to beg meat this winter."

The old woman said, "You are going to get the worst beating of your life, Slave Girl."

"No, I don't think so. I am very tired of people threatening to beat me. If you mean to do it, why don't you start? The next person who raises a stick or a whip at me will not raise anything else with that arm for a long time!"

Pea Finder, who had become senile in her mind as well as her body, said, "We don't want to beat you. We love you."

Birdy began to hack at the under jaw of the buffalo cow to get at the huge tongue, which was a delicacy when smoked and prepared right. See Dead Bull was embarrassed and uncertain. She jerked at the tail, trying to split the hide down the backbone. She said, "If we can have only one, we must make do. We should save every piece of meat we can."

"But no!" Horse Tender said. "There are more than one, Mother. I have ..." She clapped her hand over her mouth. They all stared at her. "I'm sorry. I don't ... I didn't mean to say 'Mother' I just ... I apologize. I only ... I have ... I wanted to say that I have seven down with Antelope Man's marked arrow in them."

She too was embarrassed and uncertain, incongruously towering over them on the big stallion. "I better go. The next buffalo is just beyond those trees. Number seven is away up by the bluffs just below that rocky place. I'll go butcher him out."

She wheeled and rode in the direction she had indicated.

It was a day of hard work. In camp, the workers built small fires upwind of the hanging meat, throwing on sprigs of juniper and damp leaves to make smoke and keep away the flies. Fortunately, a good frost came on the land that night. Horse Tender did not sleep. She built fires near the three buffalo that were still unskinned and rode back and forth all night protecting them. Camp dogs and coyotes and wolves gorged and fought all across the miles of hunting ground; they seemed crazy from the sight and smell of so much meat.

In the middle of the following morning Pea Finder collapsed from working too hard, as she had done several times before in the past year. Horse Tender loaded her on Smoke and led the horse into camp, where she put the old woman to bed.

Antelope Man was hobbling around keeping a small smudge fire going. He said, "That outlaw stud was walking as gentle as a children's pony."

"He wouldn't throw off anyone who is sick, Father. I wish you could have seen him yesterday in the chase. All I had to do was show him which one and he would do the rest. He would put me right in for a perfect shot. He nearly got gored twice."

"I believe you. It was a successful hunt for the whole band. From what I hear, the better hunters got five or six." He was chuckling.

"Father?"

"Yes?"

"I screamed at your mother-in-law yesterday and insulted her."

"Why did you do it?"

"Because of the way the War Club Society man treated me. And because I was worn out from excitement and riding. And I don't know how to apologize to your mother-in-law."

"In all these years," he said, "I've not learned how to apologize to her. Don't worry about it. Did you sleep last night?"

"No."

"There's a lot of work to do around here, meat to slice, more racks to build, hides to scrape. The women will be in after a while with the last of the meat. I want you to go out and guard my horse herd. Take two good robes with you. Guard them a good while. That's an order."

"Thank you, Father. Could Birdy tell Broken Ice I'm sorry I screamed and insulted her?"

"I guess so. Get going. My horse Smoke is about to drop in his tracks from weariness. After all, he and my magic bow wood from down south got seven buffaloes yesterday."

Snow lay ankle deep on the valley. It lay lightly on the limbs of trees. The bunch grass stuck up through it, and the horses could easily paw out all the natural cured hay they needed. Each afternoon the sun tried its power on the snow and left a thin crackle of ice on the surface, so that human beings and heavy animal beings made a loud crunch with every step. To look across the white terrain too much made the eyes hurt.

She had been watching Ride Away watching her for some time. He wanted to appear hidden and also to be seen. Finally he settled himself on a low rock ledge as far away as a loud voice would carry and began to work diligently on some small object in his hands. She went to him.

"Oh!" he said putting something inside his blanket. "I didn't see you."

"No, you are deaf and blind," Horse Tender said. "What is it that you are pretending to hide?"

"Pretending?"

"Yes. Everywhere I look you are hiding plain as day. What are you working on?"

"Just a string. I was making it out of horsehair, but then I decided it had to be made out of soft doeskin."

"What will you do with the string?"

"I'm making a present for my sweetheart."

"Lucky girl. You are going to give her a string. What's her name?"

"The string is only to hang it around her neck. She's mad at me right now. I want to give her a pretty piece of jewelry and maybe it will soften her heart."

"Let's see it."

He took it out and handed it to her, a white metal disc with what seemed to be a human face on one side, along with other designs. It was called a *coin* and Ride Away had traded four wolf skins for it to a warrior who had got it at the Mandan village on Big River. He had worked a hole near the edge with a knife point and obviously had been rubbing it against fur to shine it.

She said, "It's beautiful."

"Do you think it's good enough to make my sweetheart love me again?"

"You men! I'm sure she only wants some token to show what you think of her. You can't buy her love with expensive jewelry."

"Well, will you accept it?"

"I'll think about it," she said. "What did we argue about last time anyway?"

"I don't know."

"I don't remember either," she said.

They argued in those days about impossible situations—that he should come as her husband and live in the crowded lodge of Antelope Man, with no status as the man of a lodge, living with four women who were not his wives nor kin—that he should purchase her and they set up their own home, leaving her adopted parents with no hunter, he needing to marry still another wife or two for someone to do the women's work—that they marry and he do the women's work before the astonished and critical eyes of his own tribe—that she, whom, he admitted, might be a better rider and bowman than any warrior in the tribe with the possible exception of himself, give up riding and hunting altogether—that they both hunt and keep the lodge, he giving up all dreams of prestige as a famous warrior, which he had dreamed since a small boy.

They were not kind or wise in their arguments, but passionate and selfish: however, in their fights and reconciliations, they probed together with a kind of fatalism for an answer that might not exist. She finally came to an idea that might have everything or nothing to do with the answer and that Ride Away thought proved that no man can understand a woman, especially this one: she wanted to have a baby.

In those days Pea Finder spent most of her days lying in the darkened tepee. They were afraid she might die. She got all the soup and rest and warmth a person needs, but she also wanted to talk. Horse Tender spent hours over her, listening to the same story about how she could find the small sign of mice which gather and hoard peas, about how she could smell them out.

One day she said to the old woman, "Pea Finder, I want to have a baby."

She was immediately interested and rose to a sitting position, her dark eyes shining out of her shrunken face. "A boy or a girl?"

"I don't care. Just a little baby and it would grow to be a child and I would take good care of it."

"Can I hold it?" the woman asked.

"Yes. Some."

"All right. I'll tell you how to have a baby."

The old woman proceeded to tell about a spot called the Baby Place on a stream called Arrow Creek. She did not know where it was, but it was in Crow country. It was a secret pool with the footprints of children on its little sandy beaches, a dimly lighted place, and a barren woman could go there to pray and make offerings. The pool was owned by little people who had wanted never to grow up; they would take pity on a woman and send a baby if she wanted one strongly enough. The woman must leave a small bow and four arrows if she was trying for a boy, a doll if she was trying for a girl. Pea Finder was so sincere in her simple faith that a person could not help agreeing to her outrageous superstition, and she stated that prayers and offerings always worked at the Baby Place, if one wanted it strongly enough, if one could find Arrow Creek.

* * *

It was late winter, well before the ice broke on
the rivers, when the horses were so poor that a man
could count their ribs. The snow was gone except
for some shady patches and the land looked desolate. Into camp one afternoon came a strange Crow
woman carrying a dead baby.

The woman, tired and near hysterical, would
only say, "Go help us," and something about
Streaked Hair.

Some of them gently took the lifeless baby from
her; others ran toward the ridge in the direction she
had pointed. They could see nothing. Those gathered near the woman said, "Get some food; she's
starving," "I know her; she's from Chickadee's
band," "That Sioux Streaked Hair has attacked
them," "Make lots of food," "We have to ride east
and find them." Meanwhile, Horse Tender, without orders from the chiefs, ran out of camp to capture the horse Smoke and then drove into the center of the village all the riding horses and pack
horses that were nearby. Before sunset a large party of men and women were mounted to ride east in
the direction the woman had pointed when she
said, "Go help us."

Later, when the legends began, this would be the
earliest action they would tell in detail about Horse
Tender. They would call it "the night we found the
remnants of Chickadee's band, after the attack by
Streaked Hair." They would say, "We called her
Horse Tender then," and one still older would say,
"We even called her Slave Girl; she was a captive,
you know." And the legend beginners would say,
"Now, this is not the Smoke you're thinking about;
that's Little Smoke. This is his sire. This is the
older brother of Spotted Pup, the great warhorse,

about ten years older from the same mare. This first Smoke, everybody thought he was an outlaw."

As among all people, the Crows built legends by a pattern. Parents had a hard time telling their children anything serious. If they said, "When I was young," the children seemed dubious and rebellious and more inclined to listen to their grandparents, who would spoil them. After time had passed and the parents had given up on telling the serious recent past, and when the children had children of their own, the children would come back and ask, "How was it when you were young?" After their first surprise, the parents would try to put it into words, how it was, especially the dramatic parts, only to find that their own parents and aunts and uncles corrected the stories according to their own lights. Whereupon the parents would turn to their grandchildren and pet them and spoil them and tell them how it was. At some point the parents would realise that they were no longer parents, but the oldest living generation, most of their own age gone, and they would reach for immortality in the lives of their descendants and the offspring of their brothers and sisters and cousins. They would look at dim memories and talk. All generations had their turn. If they took liberty with the facts, it was in the interest of whatever truth their long years had given.

The legends would say that Horse Tender mounted on Smoke was the first that night to find the straggling procession of Chickadee's people. That she first brought a load of them safely to the village, four, one dead and three alive. That she charged back east a dozen times, with Smoke running like a racehorse, to search them out in the darkness and bring them home, walking on the way back, the black horse following as gentle as a puppy without so much as a rope around his neck. Legend put as many as six of the starving refuges on his back at once as he followed the young woman. But legends exaggerate; in fact, at that time it was still true that only people of little consequence in the band saw anything unusual about Horse Tender and the chiefs probably did not even know her name.

Next day they cared for the ninety-seven survivors of Chickadee's band, which were all that remained alive of three or four times that number, who had been surprised by the Sioux attack a week earlier. Many of them had some wounds. Chickadee himself had an arrow wound in his arm and severely cut and bruised feet from the long walk.

Also there were five dead, including the baby. These bodies had to be wrapped and prepared for burial in trees or on scaffolds. The work was done by several women of High Owl's band, for those of Chickadee's band were too weak. Horse Tender represented Antelope Man's lodge in the work.

She showed up at her own lodge at midday, went inside, and grabbed from the wall a half doeskin without asking anyone. It was soft tanned and whitened by rubbing with clay. She did not even look at them as she took it. A few minutes later she was back, empty-handed but obviously agitated and uncertain.

She suddenly screamed at them: "I want some beads! I want something pretty!"

They stared at her in surprise, not understanding. Broken Ice, See Dead Bull, and Birdy were cooking a large pot of stew for the refugees.

She did not look like a slave nor a little girl as she went on screaming: "I want colored beads! You hear me? I want a pretty thing! What is it? Just because it's little, it doesn't matter? It had as much right to live as anyone!"

She suddenly became silent and took down from its hanging place on a limb just outside the door the rawhide box that was her private place to keep her clothes. She rummaged through it, then ran back to where the women prepared the bodies.

Into the tiny stiff fist she put the soft string with the. *coin* attached—the shined white metal—that when the small spirit went away on the wind it might carry a token to show how someone considered it important and loved it in the first world where it lived.

9. The Fourth Wolf

During the Moon when Sage Hens Dance the council of High Owl's band met almost daily and runners left camp or returned with messages from other Crow bands. They were planning a strike against the Sioux.

Rainy, a leader with a good fighting record, had passed the pipe for war, and many warriors had smoked. Then everyone realized that the matter needed further consideration. Above all, no Crow camp should be left unprotected. Competent chiefs and warriors must remain behind to stand guard and defend their own women and children. The threat from the east and southeast was uncertain, but could not be ignored.

Some of the messengers from other bands who sat in council proposed that the strike be put off until midsummer, when the horses would be fat and the whole thing could be carefully organized. Rainy would have none of it. They had reliable information that Streaked Hair was now camped near where Little Boggy runs into Cheyenne River. Some Crows still living remember that camp spot. The thing was to outguess the Sioux. If Streaked Hair was planning a strong push west, he undoubtedly would take time raising his forces and many of them might want to wait for better grass. The thing was to hit him before he was ready and at a place where he would be risking his own women and children.

Rainy asserted that he wanted a fast force of experienced warriors to go without delay, and the council reluctantly gave its unanimous consent. He enlisted 101 men, about half from two other bands and half from High Owl's band, with only Chickadee from the recently decimated band. The men gathered extra arrows and extra moccasins; the women packed pouches of pemmican for them. Each would take two war-horses.

As they prepared for the war dance that evening two opposite ideas hung over the people of the camp. With all Rainy's war honors and considering the experience of the braves going with him, how could any stand against them? The opposing awareness was this: what a small group to be riding so far into Sioux country! The war dance had a purpose; it would ease any sadness and apprehension. Also, it was a commitment to an understanding; this was no raid for plunder; it was for the Crow Nation.

They danced to the drum in the light of a huge fire, the warriors' faces painted with spots and lines of red and yellow and white. Some warriors worked themselves into a frenzy of stamping and yelling; the spectators answered their cries. At midnight Rainy's party mounted their waiting horses and thundered out of camp. It was well understood that they would travel in daytime and sleep at night, but it was necessary that they hit the war trail while the spirit was strong upon them, not so much for their own sake as for those they left behind.

It was quiet in camp in the following days, with a kind of determined patience; but all was confusion in the Antelope Man household. Horse Tender had gone hunting and had not come back. She had been gone too long. She had not been staying away more than one night recently.

Antelope Man hobbled out to hunt his horses and returned disconsolate. The women knew that he was crabby when his foot hurt, but See Dead Bull asked him how his horses were getting along.

He said, "My two best horses are missing, the bay and the big black stud."

Broken Ice said, "Tell your husband I knew it would happen. That Slave Girl has stolen his best horses and gone back to her people. I think she stole some pemmican too."

They all stared at her without much sympathy. Antelope Man said, "I don't see how she could steal any pemmican; she killed every speck of meat in the lodge."

Pea Finder raised up from her pallet and said, "Horse Tender did not run away. She will come back soon."

The assertion seemed to reassure him and Antelope Man said, "Of course she didn't run away. She knows I would worry. She'll probably be back tomorrow."

Two days later he went hunting afoot, thinking maybe to surprise a deer or at least a couple of rabbits, but came home hours later empty-handed. The women refrained from comment on his hunt.

Pea Finder said, "Horse Tender will come back.

She knows how much meat we have, and she'll come home before we starve."

He burst out at them, "Why did you beat her so much? I told you not to! Now wonder she ran off, the way she was treated!"

Old Broken Ice said to her eldest daughter, "Your husband cannot make up his mind. Day before yesterday he was sure she would come back."

See Dead Bull said, "We have not beat her in years."

"You used to!" he insisted. "You treated her worse than a dog! A sorry dog would run off if he was done that way!"

Birdy said, "I helped her make a dress not long ago. She's not mad at me."

"Then why has she run off?" Antelope Man demanded.

Birdy seemed about to start crying.

See Dead Bull, standing as solid as a rounding boulder, said, "All I have ever tried to do is make a respectable lodge. I just want things to be right. I'm a hard worker. If I've done wrong, it was only because I want to keep a proper lodge."

Pea Finder said, "She'll come back before we starve."

"Who's starving?" he asked. "Don't you think I can hunt? I could trade a horse for meat till my foot gets better! No one ever went hungry in my lodge! But I want my daughter back! You hear me? My daughter! That's what I called her!"

"She'll come back," Pea Finder said.

Antelope Man looked at her savagely, but then seemed to change his attitude. He said defiantly to his older wife, "That's right! She'll come back! You wait and see!"

* * *

As they moved into what was clearly enemy country, Rainy reorganized his scouting, putting Elk Head in charge of that function during night time. They were traveling fast, but trying to find each day a place where the new grass was showing, to let the horses graze awhile. When they were on the move, Rainy kept three or more guards fanned out ahead of them in sight. The day guards had no regular schedule, for they had the duty of getting fresh meat whenever the opportunity came. At sundown each day Rainy chose a double campsite, one place to build fires and eat, another two long arrow flights away for sleeping.

Elk Head set up a plan for the night guard, using only Fox Society men, three wolves out till midnight, three more till dawn. The first night after he took charge he could not sleep. He got up and walked among the still forms in the sleeping camp, then became aware that two others were also awake, Rainy and Chickadee. The three of them talked casually in monotones, pausing sometimes to hear the sound of their wolves far out on the high ground in the darkness.

At about midnight Elk Head awakened the three morning wolves and sent them out. A short time later one of the evening wolves came in. He said, "Is that you, Rainy? Elk Head said three. Then he sent four."

Approaching, Elk Head asked, "What's the trouble?"

"There were four wolves out there. Why didn't you tell us?"

"No, only three."

"But I heard three others besides me; there were four."

"You're hearing things," said Elk Head. "Get some sleep."

The second man came in and reported the same thing, a fourth wolf.

"You heard an echo," Rainy said.

"No, it couldn't have been."

"It was an animal, a coyote or wolf," Elk Head said.

"No, I know what I heard. It was guarding this camp."

Chickadee said, "I don't like this at all. It's a bad omen."

The third evening wolf came in and confirmed what the other two had heard.

Chickadee's voice had become a hoarse exaggerated whisper, which was more likely to awaken the sleeping warriors than a normal speaking voice. "It's *Napa!* God's helper!" he said. "It's a bad sign!"

Rainy and Elk Head tried to quieten him, then walked him a distance out away from those who were still asleep. "It's *E-saca wata,*" he said. "Old Man Coyote himself! It's an omen for us to turn around and go back!"

Elk Head said, "If it's *E-saca wata,* that's a good omen. He's going to help us."

"It's no kind of omen," Rainy said. "Listen, there's an explanation for this."

Chickadee insisted, "Three of them heard it! It's not natural! We're fools to ride deeper into Lakota territory with so few warriors! This is a bad sign!"

"It's a natural happening and will be explained," Rainy said. "The three wolves who reported it were mistaken."

Elk Head said quickly, "The Fox men are not mistaken!"

"Now wait," Rainy said. "Calm down. Listen to me a minute. The men that smoked for this raid knew exactly what we planned to do. We're a small, fast fighting group, and every man is experienced. I'd rather have a hundred men like this than ten times as many who are disorganized and troubled by dissention."

"I don't like it," Chickadee said. "How many of us will get through it safely? How many of us will go back alive?"

"Are you worried?"

"I'm telling you that Streaked Hair has a reputation for clever fighting. He will surround an enemy before they know what'a happening. I know his power! And now this bad omen!"

Rainy said, "Streaked Hair is a man just like you and me. He would like us to think he's a great general, and he would like us to fear him. What we're going to do is swoop down on him like an eagle and take his scalp, then all go home."

"What about this fourth wolf? It's a bad sign!"

Elk Head interjected, "It's a good sign. I think Chief Chickadee should go back. He has no following here. He should leave us while it's still safe."

"I won't go back!"

"Then listen to me," Rainy said. "I cannot have a chief talking among the men if that chief has no confidence. All the men are going to hear about the fourth wolf. I ask you to leave us and go back, or else keep your mouth shut."

"I won't go back," he said. "Both of you don't understand, but I won't go back. My band is broken, ruined! I'm a Crow and not a coward."

Elk Head said, "You don't sound like a Crow to me. The unseen persons and powers are on our side."

"Think on that," he said, "when you ride safely home without me. And leave my body for foreign women to cut me up."

"Wait now," Rainy said. "This has gone far enough. We will take home the scalp of Streaked Hair. I say that. What else is to be said?"

"I don't like it," Chickadee answered.

"Then listen my friend, my brother. I want to hear it for the last time right here and now. I have these men who smoked with me for this raid. You are not the leader, nor you." He put up his hand to stop Elk Head's interruption. "No, wait. I'll have an end to this my way. You cannot say 'I don't like it' to my warriors. You can believe that the fourth wolf is natural or magic or whatever. I don't care. I am Chief right now. You can turn back or you can be quiet, but if you put fear and doubt in the minds of my men, I'll kill you."

Chickadee said stubbornly, "I don't like it."

"You don't have to like it. We heard you say it. We understand you. That's it. If you put fear and doubt in the minds of my men, I'll kill you with my own hand."

Chickadee said nothing.

Rainy said, "Get some sleep. I want to get over into the headwaters of Boggy Creek tomorrow. Then we'll move fast."

The following day clouds formed and lowered and became a solid gray covering. The second watch had also heard an extra wolf voice in the darkness; and they heard it the next night and the night after.

Boggy Creek drained wasteland in its western reaches, red clay hillocks and banks and dry gullies. Little but prickly-pear cactus and sagebrush grew. Farther on, mottes of trees appeared, then a broad uneven band of cottonwoods and willows and shinnery flanking the winding stream. As Rainy's band pushed on, the sky lowered more and a mist began to fall. The silted flats became boggy. The horses' hoofs kicked up bits and clods of mud.

Rainy mounted early and rode among the awakening men. They saw that he had renewed his warpaint and wore a tuft of eagle feathers in his hair. "This is the day," he said. "Catch your strongest horse. We'll run into their horse tenders and guards very soon, and their village by midday. Take no prisoners. Steal nothing. I want dead Lakotas!

"By tomorrow morning we'll be back here. Move fast! We want one scalp. That of a chief, with a white streak in it; they also say he wears small copper bells in his hair.

"Wounded! Should any man be wounded, he must continue to ride. Tie him on his horse if need be.

"Now! Grab a bite to eat and let's ride! We are Crow warriors!"

A short time later they rode down the valley in a trot. Some had painted their faces, and the mist streaked them. It was a wintery day for the Moon of New Leaves. The riders became tense and silent.

When they saw Sioux horses, the raiders spread out in order better to scout the terrain. They found a near-grown boy and killed him with arrows, hardly pausing, then two other horse tenders escaped over the low hills. Rainy waved his line of men into a gallop. The mounts ran heavily in the

mud. Chickadee, riding near the leader, shouted
that the village was still too far away for such a
gait. Seeing the labor and heaving of the horses,
Rainy pulled back to a trot. He scanned the hills
for enemy scouts.

The battle that day, from the Crow standpoint,
was in two parts: when Rainy was trying to attack,
and when Rainy was trying to save as many of his
men as possible.

First the enemy appeared behind him, some
twenty warriors, dangerous Sioux in feathered
headdresses. The Crow leader ignored his excited
men, who wanted to turn and pursue, and kept his
steady trot toward where the village must lie. But
he soon struck a point of trees where Sioux lay in
wait with guns. He lost two men there, shot clean
out of their saddles, before he whipped into a run
and veered across the small stream.

They saw two other parties of enemy riders.
Chickadee screamed, "We're surrounded! They're
everywhere!"

Elk Head, with some two dozen men, charged
and scattered the enemy. Rainy led his men
through in a dead run. They held to the open
timber and the edges of the foothill for good footing; the silted flats were impossible now. On a rise,
the Crows could see the gray hanging smoke of the
village merging with the ever-lowering clouds. The
mist thickened.

From three sides came charges of howling
Lakotas. Those in front were as many as the
Crows. Rainy tried to fold his line in and find cov-
er. As those enemy charging in front passed a loop-
ing bend of the stream, a strange thing happened.
The leader threw up his arms and was pitched

headfirst from his running horse. Others fell. Rainy
was still telling his men to hold their fire, but the
Sioux were falling. How could it be?

Rainy's men scattered, for there was no decent
cover at hand. They tried to keep in sight, still moving down the valley. Chickadee screamed again,
"They're all around us!" Then he died, a dozen arrows in himself and his horse from a concentration
of Sioux in the brush.

Possibly it was the death of Chickadee that
started the second phase of the battle in Rainy's
mind—to save such of his men as he could. The
fighting became hectic. The mist turned to rain,
which seemed to be falling through a layer of fog.
It seemed eerie to them, the screams of horses as if
begging their human masters, the muffled thunder
of hoofs on the wet earth, the dull boom of the few
guns, and the stench of powder smoke.

Rainy tried to take them out through the hills to
the north, but found his way blocked. He turned
back upstream through the timber, trying to keep
them within his sight or hearing. He had lost a
dozen good men.

He was stopped before a bend of the small
stream, where the high silt banks hid clusters of
enemy. The Crows were in a cross fire from other
enemies to the left in the timber. While Rainy was
deciding to charge, those behind the banks ran and
scattered sooner than they needed to. Beneath the
banks, he saw pools of blood being washed away
by the rain, then two Lakota dead in the gravel,
then three more. The arrows had been pulled from
their fresh wounds. One enemy man was scalped,
his head brilliant red, for the rain would not let the
blood clot and darken, a large man with a fancy

porcupine quill frontpiece on his chest.

Rainy thrust up the valley. He counted as many as three hundred Sioux on the hills on either side. "Go through!" he shouted. "Don't stop for anything!" It was difficult to judge either the disposition of his own men or that of the enemy in the heavy mist. Some of his warriors bogged their horses so badly that they scrambled off and ran afoot.

They had camped at the same spot as the night before, which seemed years in the past. Elk Head went out about midnight to where Rainy wandered sleepless. He cleared his throat to announce himself and asked, "What do you think happened?"

"Leave me alone," Rainy said.

"Now wait a minute. I'm not blaming you. None of the warriors will blame you. Twenty-nine men gone. The Lakota lost more than that; I counted that many myself. We expect to lose men. We have to pay a price for our land."

"Leave me alone," Rainy said.

"But Chief Chickadee wanted to die. He lost his family and his band. He expected to die. No one blames you. You've lost warriors before."

"Leave me alone."

"We'll defend you in the council, Rainy. This raid accomplished its mission. The Lakota know they've been hit. They'll mourn their dead and think twice. No one blames you."

Rainy said, "Go wake your morning wolves and leave me alone."

"I've sent them out already." Elk Head's voice dropped to a hoarse whisper. "It's out there again, Rainy, behind us now. Guarding our back trail.

We ran into a hornet's nest. The fourth wolf saved us. It was a good omen, Rainy."

"Leave me alone," he said.

Antelope Man had been thinking all night. Not so much about the returned raiders, the wild stories of the battle, the wailing of kin, the recriminations, the praise and bragging. Perhaps it was because he could not be so excited as some of the others. Perhaps he had not been thinking at all, but only wandering around in the dark.

The clouds had broken and cleared. The stars shined through. You should have seen her back then. She remembered every word I told her about the stars. Smart as a whip! Things it took a man years to learn, then you turn around twice and find out she's been looking and understanding on her own, and knows more than you do about the heavens.

You should have seen her at first. Ten years old. A skinny little girl. A spitfire! Smart! Never forgot a single thing she ever heard. Same way about arrows. I taught her a little about horses, so she got more horse medicine than any man in camp.

I'm an old fool. I know that. She couldn't have been so bright as I thought. It could not be true that she grew up to be the most beautiful Crow woman who ever lived. It was because she called me "father." I did protect her some and teach her some. I hope she'll remember me when she sees a star.

He sat down on a patch of spring grass, sometimes with his face in his hands, sometimes with his eyes up at the sky, which was lighting as dawn approached.

"Father, are you awake?"

At some age men do not admit to others that they are old, but they see times of evidence in themselves. He was remembering when he thought she was drowned in the flooding river, and she asked that; memory and hearing get confused.

"Father, are you asleep?"

He spoke to his memory. "No."

"I got a buffalo, but didn't carry it all. Your bay warhorse is played out and your black stud is weary. I only brought one hindquarter and the hump ribs and tongue. I was ashamed to load them heavy."

Then she asked, "Father?"

"Yes?"

"Can I ask a favor?"

"All right."

"Don't make me give an explanation. Please?"

"All right."

"Don't cry, Father. Please don't. Does your foot hurt? I'll make a hot bath for it—hot, then cool, hot, then cool. It will ease the pain. You'll see. I'll rub it with bear grease salve. Please don't cry, Father. Everything will be all right."

He followed her and helped hang up the fresh meat she had brought. Inside the tepee the other women were stirring. Horse Tender took the horse-leg water bags, slung them across her shoulder, went after the morning supply of water.

10. The Baby Place

The reputation of Horse Tender was spreading among her adopted people because she brought meat to those lodges whose hunters were sick or unlucky. The Crows were generous with one another, but some of the men felt shame in asking for meat, even some of the women. Horse Tender would go to them as privately as possible and ask if they would please try to find a use for some extra meat. They did not seem to mind taking a pack load of dressed elk or bighorn or antelope from her.

See Dead Bull and her mother fussed about giving away meat, for it might have been traded for property of some kind. The lodge was not so prosperous as it would have been had they got more buffalo skins.

When one of the soldier societies supervised a big hunt, Horse Tender avoided trouble by holding back and remaining inconspicuous. But she often lost her temper at the unfairness. If the escaping herd held together, she might find it impossible to make a single kill. Then she would come back to the lodge furious, planning her own hunt in the opposite direction the following day. Ride Away would try to give her fresh meat, but not the skins, so she would refuse.

Most of the skins she brought home were deer, elk, and antelope. Chicago would not trade for these; they had to be bartered away to other Indians. Thus while other lodges traded their prime buffalo robes for white man goods, Antelope Man's women had to watch with envy. Antelope Man began to trade horses for goods. He got himself a short gun, which could be stuck in a man's belt, also needed iron things such as knives, scrapers, arrowpoints, axes, and pots. But no salt, sugar, coffee, beads. While Horse Tender was giving away meat, they saw the luxuries go to more prosperous families and saw their horse herd shrink.

Chicago was preparing packs for a pack train to the mouth of Elk River. He would join with traders from other Crow bands and would return in about a month. Horse Tender was helping him, as were his two children, in pressing down the skins and robes so that they could be bound tightly.

She asked him whether he believed in magic and offerings and whether he knew the location of Arrow Creek.

"Well," he said, "they's lots of strange things happen, Little Gal. I know whereabouts Arrow Creek is. High Owl and the council will like as not move us there before long, because the wood is getting scarce here. I hope I get back before we move. But what's this magic and offerings stuff?"

"I want to have a baby."

"Magic stuff is hard to figure. . . . What? You want to have what?"

"A baby. You told me when I was a little girl

that I could ask you questions and you would explain to me."

"Explain! . . . Told you! . . . Good law a-mighty, Little Gal! You got to be married first."

"Now, Chicago, I expected a better answer than that from you."

"Why, you do! You got to get married."

"Now, Chicago."

"No, you got to . . . good law a-mighty! Listen, Little Gal, it takes male and female. You know the flowers . . . little bees come around and . . . well . . ."

"Chicago, are you going to explain things like that to me at my age?"

He said to his half-grown son and daughter. "Go on swimming, like you wanted to. I don't need you any more this evening. Come back before dark."

When they were gone Horse Tender told him, "I have a lover, Chicago."

"Who is it?"

"You don't need to know, you old gossip. He can certainly make a woman pregnant, and I don't know what's wrong."

"Little Gal, you don't want a baby. How could you take care of one and all the running around and hunting you do? I know who kills all the skins Antelope Man gets."

"Pea Finder would help take care of it."

"That old woman's dying. I've seen them dry up like that. She ain't long for this world."

"Oh, nonsense, Chicago. Birdy would help. Antelope Man would love to have a baby around."

"Is it Antelope Man's? Would it be his child?"

"Of course not! He's my father."

"Don't get mad. I just asked. Little Gal, you got a strange situation at best. I like you, but I don't see no easy way for your life, doing the way you do. At the post where Elk River runs into Big River is a doctor. I reckon he's there yet. He's a sort of white medicine man is what he is. They know about these things. I'll ask him about it, but I don't put no great hope in what he says."

When Chicago returned, he first gave small gifts of sugar to High Owl, One Good Eye, Rainy, Elk Head, and other important lodges; then he found Horse Tender and took her aside.

"I talked to the doctor, Little Gal. Then I talked to women. I can't talk to women around here; they're my own people. But I asked Mandan and Minnetaree women. They all agree."

"You're the greatest friend in the world," she said. "I knew I could count on you. What did they say?"

"They said the same as the doctor. Little Gal, you got to quit riding horseback."

"No, I mean about having a baby."

"Yes, Little Gal, you got to quit riding horse-back."

"Quit saying that! I did not ask for advice about how to run my life. I asked how to grow a baby inside me."

"You got to stop riding horseback. I've seen you ride. Like a maniac. You ride every day."

"What are you saying? Women work! They drag wood! They pull driftwood out of the river! They ride! They lie with men and have babies! I hate your white doctor! He's stupid! And those foreign women! I hate them all!"

"Little Gal, I'm only trying to help you."

"Stop calling me pet names! You men! Cut off

my head and then I will enjoy life more! I hate you!"

"I don't hate you," he said.

"Stop being kind to me! You men! Quit riding horseback, you say! You men! It's not *Magahawathus*, man alone! It's *Ah-bah-daht-deah!* The Creator! You think he made horses for you to ride? He made them to take the burden off women! Horses obey women better!"

"Some horses obey some women better. I only tell you what they told me."

"I hate them all! I hate you too! I'll never sell you another skin, raw or tanned! I hope you go broke and starve! My father, Antelope Man, will punch you right in the nose!"

"It won't be the first time I got hit," he said. "Please don't be mad at me, Little Gal. I done give away half the profits of my trip. You can take the other half. Bring you a pack horse to my lodge and choose what you want. I don't hate you at all."

"But you don't understand," she said.

"I understand you asked me once 'What's wrong with trouble?' This ain't the end of it. It's trouble now and trouble down the road."

"But you don't understand, Chicago. You really don't. It's about pain. Also tedious work. Men do it in the Sun Dance on purpose in front of everyone. They torture themselves. It's to show their sincerity. You have wanted to release them and I have too. It's struggle for more than just eat and sleep and stay warm. We are more than that, men and women too. We have to find out. Oh, Chicago, don't you know that women do it! Pain is the only personal thing we have. We want to swell up and have pain and make a new person. The little thing is innocent. It doesn't know about the pain and tedious trouble. It takes years of tenderness and care, but it is a new person."

Chicago had listened carefully to her harangue, but had, without moving, seemed to back off into his own thoughts. He said, "Little Gal, did you go with Rainy's raid into Sioux country?"

"That's not what I asked you to help me with," she said. "I asked you how I could conceive a baby. That's all I wanted to know."

"Quit riding horseback."

"I won't quit. I'll prove you wrong. You'll see. Time will prove that you are mistaken."

"Time won't get no cherry," he said. "I ain't no virgin. I just go on what I hear and see and what I figure out in my mind."

Every tuft of buffalo grass was a barrier for Pea Finder to cross. She paused before a bush of scrub oak, tottered, nearly ran into it, got herself turned. Horse Tender said, "It's too far. It's too hard for you. Give me directions and I can find it by myself."

The old woman said, "No. It's all right. We are nearly there. See the sandstone ledge?"

"Do you want me to carry you?"

"No."

"Then let's rest again," Horse Tender said.

They sat on the grass, and Pea Finder clutched the small doll she carried to her shrunken chest as if it were a baby. The doll was made of leather with beads on it and tiny moccasins and horse mane for hair. Horse Tender carried in her hands a hoop of willow and a chasing stick and a toy bow, with four arrows, well made.

The old woman asked, "Did you have a doll

when you were little?"

"Yes, I had two. The boy doll was named Brave Rider, and the girl doll, who was very fancy, I named Pink Morning."

Pea Finder said, "I had lots of dolls, but I only remember one name. He was made out of a corncob and had a clay head and his head got broke, so his name was Broken Head. I loved him."

In a moment the old woman asked, "Don't you really care whether it's a boy or a girl?"

"No, I don't. But I was wondering what to say when I leave the toys."

"It doesn't matter. Except don't say it loud. Just whisper or say it inside yourself. The little persons will know. They can see you made the doll moccasins and the arrowpoints and everything, carefully. They will understand."

Horse Tender helped her up and they went on. The Baby Place lay under the sandstone ledge, hidden so well that one could hardly find it without knowing its location. From one direction it was blocked by marshy brakes of willow sprouts, from other directions by dense growths of sumac and shinnery and scrub cedar. Pea Finder kept getting caught in brambles. Finally, they came into the open under the ledge and saw the clear pool of water.

It seemed not to be fed by a spring, but perhaps a seep through the earth. It was quiet and as dim as twilight. It smelled damp. They moved silently back under the rock ceiling. Horse Tender laid the bow and arrows, the hoop and chasing stick, and the doll in a careful row on the beach by the water. She whispered, "I promise if I can have a baby I will be a good mother. I swear that I'm only twenty-six winters, not too young and not too old, and have a large heart toward children."

On the way back to camp, Horse Tender had to
carry Pea Finder. The old woman was as light as a
child of eight winters.

They had moved up west into the mountains to
camp with two other Crow bands. The high valleys
provided rich grazing where they widened,
meadows with clumps of aspen trees. In the rocky
canyons grew scrub juniper and on the slopes,
thick stands of lodgepole pine. The tops of the
mountains were rounded with snow, shiny in the
sunlight, and the water in springs and seeps and
small creeks was icy cold.

One of the neighboring Crow camps had trouble
over a woman, who was called Bad Woman. Her
origin was uncertain, though she undoubtedly had
been a captive or a runaway from another tribe.
Before she came to the Crows, her husband had
suspected her of sexual infidelity and had mutilated
her by cutting off the end of her nose. Recently the
Crow women had begun to criticize her behavior,
and the neighboring band had banished her at the
insistence of a henpecked council member. She
would go away one evening and show up the very
next morning at some lodge fire to beg for food.
Bad Woman's situation and her stubbornness were
the subject of much gossip around the camps.

One afternoon Horse Tender came down the rim
of a canyon toward camp, leading Smoke, who carried the meat and skin of a bighorn sheep. Voices
came to her through the gnarled junipers, one of
them that of Chicago.

"What good is it to kill yourself? Don't you
know other people have trouble too?"

"What do you care?"

"I don't care a damn! That's a fact! But who will mourn you? Nobody! Who will feel sorry for you? You ain't got but one life! One time on the face of this earth! Throw it away! It ain't none of my business, woman!"

He saw Horse Tender approaching and, hardly pausing in his tirade, said, "There's another one as stubborn as you are! I hope to hell the Good Lord understands women, because I sure don't!"

They were standing on a ledge of white rock overlooking a stony, broken bluff—any person who fell off it would surely be killed.

Bad Woman said, "You're right about one thing. Women are worse than men."

Though it was not cold she wore a thin woven blanket over her shoulders and held it up with one hand to cover all her face except her eyes. She was of indeterminate age, well past thirty.

At the remark about women, Chicago railed at her: "Women are not worse than men! It's hardheaded stubbornness! My little wife is the best person in a hundred miles of here! She's uglier than you are and ain't even got her nose cut off! But she's got love and charity and decency! She's worth more in her little finger than all the chiefs and warriors! Don't you understand me at all? Some of you redskins are nearly as crazy as white people!"

Bad Woman said, "I don't know what it has to do with me."

Horse Tender said, "Can you use some fresh meat, Chicago?"

"I don't care," he said. "Give some to my wife and tell her I said give you some coffee if you want to. But I wish you would talk to this female here. She don't want to live. I told her she can stay at my lodge and I won't touch her. She could work for my little woman, who is a damned easy person to work for. All she's got to do is keep her nose clean. I mean . . ." He stopped in embarrassment.

Bad Woman said in a low, calm voice, "Too many people come around your tepee all the time. I couldn't live there."

Chicago asked Horse Tender, "Will you talk to her? I got to go make a trade. I'm late now."

"Go ahead," Horse Tender told him.

"Will you talk to her?"

"Yes."

When he had gone, the two women studied each other. Bad Woman's eyes held a questioning appeal. Horse Tender said, "Couldn't you find your people you grew up with? Your kin?"

"I couldn't go to them."

"Why not?"

"Because. You wouldn't understand."

"I might. Tell me."

"I was a handsome girl. I had lots of suitors. I couldn't go back there looking the way I do."

"I understand."

In a moment Horse Tender said, "You don't need to hold your blanket over your face. I don't mind how you look. Let me see."

"No."

"Why not?"

"Because I'm afraid to die. When you see me and hate me, then I don't have anyone else to turn to."

"Do you want to come to my lodge and live?"

"Yes, but I don't think it's possible."

"Why not?"

"Are you the head of your lodge?"

Horse Tender hesitated. She stepped back to Smoke, who was picking at the tough bunch grass, and petted him.

Bad Woman repeated, "Are you the head of your lodge?"

"Do you want a friend?"

"Yes," Bad Woman said, "I think you are the last chance I have left. I'd be already gone if the trader had not come and talked to me."

"Well then, listen. I'm the head of my lodge, but I wouldn't do anything to hurt the pride of my father or mother. Also, in my rawhide box I have a thing which will make me a chief in the band, but I'm not ready."

At these words Bad Woman frowned as if questioning their truth, but her brown eyes still contained the silent appeal, "What is the thing?"

"A certain enemy scalp. Are you a good worker?"

"Yes. I can dig roots and tan skins and drag wood and dry meat and everything. I work hard."

"Do you chase men?"

"No, I do not. I did wrong, but now I only want to be near friends and do work and have a place where I belong."

"If you want to come and live at my lodge, let me see your face."

After some hesitation, Bad Woman dropped the blanket to her shoulders. Her nostrils were elongated from the mutilation; otherwise her features were regular. She had probably been pretty as a girl.

Horse Tender said, "It doesn't look as bad as you imagine. It will be a favor to me if you don't hide your face from me. I think well of you after seeing it. Hide when you feel you must, but not from me."

"Do you really think I could live at your lodge?"

"You can. It will be hard at first. It will seem

impossible. It will take several moons to understand. At first, you will think I lie when I say I'm the head of the lodge. But think twice, and three times, and still again. Please do not blame my mother, See Dead Bull, too much. You will find friends and a place to belong."

Bad Woman asked, "What if they tell me to leave?"

"You must do what I tell you! And have patience."

"I don't want to die," Bad Woman said. "I was afraid to. To get broken on the rocks. I want to trust you."

Horse Tender said hesitantly and slowly, "I think the easiest creature to deal with is game. They are here for us, and easy. Next is animals like horses. Next harder is enemies. The hardest of all is friends. They take patience and long kindness. I should not talk so much about it."

"I want to go with you," Bad Woman said. "Come on."

They picked their way through the rocks and trees down to High Owl's camp. At the lodge, Horse Tender put the woman to unpacking the meat, then went straightway to Antelope Man, and told him, "She will work for us. She has no place to go, but she's a good worker."

See Dead Bull quickly entered the conversation. "That's Bad Woman. She will not sleep in the tepee with me and my sister and our husband."

Horse Tender said, "She wants to sleep outside under the brush arbor. She's a hard worker at gathering wood and everything."

"Yes," Antelope Man said, "she will have to sleep under the brush arbor."

Broken Ice said, "Ask your husband what will

she do when it rains? And when winter comes?"

The woman had expertly tied a cloth rag about the lower part of her face, hiding her nose. She was carefully arranging the new meat on the meat rack.

Horse Tender said, "If it rains, I will get skins for another small tepee, so we won't be so crowded."

"You will get skins? That's a laugh," See Dead Bull said. "We don't have enough buffalo skins now. Robes are the best for trading, and every family has more than us. We sure don't need another worker to tan skins!"

"I will get skins," Horse Tender insisted.

"When? When we have traded off all our horses and don't have a stitch of clothes on our back?"

"Before that. I will get skins for robes."

Broken Ice said, "Tell your husband this Slave Girl is trying to rule the lodge."

Antelope Man said, "I am the man around here. I don't like so much argument. I say that Bad Woman must sleep under the brush arbor unless it rains and she has to work hard and obey orders."

Pea Finder died that winter. That she and other old ones passed away did not seem a result of the cold, for they were well cared for; it was merely that the white, careless spirit of winter favored death and made them wait so long for spring that they forgot to hope. Horse Tender put in the body wrappings a cupful of tiny peas she traded for along with the old woman's digging stick and hide scraper. Birdy and See Dead Bull put in beads. Even Broken Ice, perhaps suspecting her own mortality, put in a good dress, with elk teeth and fur trimming.

Also that winter the big black mother of Smoke,

gaunt from poor nourishment and pregnant, was dragged down by a pack of wolves. The sign in the snow showed how she had been ganged up on, followed, harassed, pulled down, eaten. Horse Tender got Ride Away to go wolf hunting with her. They killed a dozen of the great shaggy doglike creatures, catching them in the bloody snow around their kills. Once she started to finish off a great bitch that already had an arrow through her chest, and kept beating the creature after it was well dead. Ride Away yelled, "Stop, Stop," and looked at her as if he were almost afraid of his hunting companion. He could not tell whether the water on her cheeks was tears or melted snow.

The mare had left her blood in the horse herds of the northern plains, not only through the stud Smoke, but through another that would be more famous as a warhorse. She had mated with a paint and the colt was spotted dark bay and white. Horse Tender and Ride Away had named him Spotted Pup, because he was like a puppy in obedience and friendliness. But now, a two-year-old, he could already outrun his older brother Smoke, who had seen a dozen winters. The other descendant in Antelope Man's herd was a get of Smoke, a half-grown colt who looked exactly like his sire. He had been named Little Smoke and was bidding fair for an outlaw image like his father.

In these days Ride Away was troubled by his lack of progress as a warrior. He was proud that with his best horse he could half the time outrun Horse Tender up on Smoke, but he would not race against Spotted Pup. The love affair was as impossible and stormy as ever.

11. The Fight at the Fort

It was late in the summer when High Owl's band moved down the valley of the *Gros Cornu* toward the rebuilt trading post at its mouth. In the points of timber, herds of elk half hid themselves, and the edges of the stream were marked by the hoofprints of much game. The post stood in the clear on a rise above the high-water mark, but since the season of flooding was well past, the band camped beside the river, well within musket range of the stockade. Two raiding parties were out, but half the warriors and most of the important leaders were present, and they did not expect any trouble with enemies at this location.

Grazing being poor, as always in the vicinity of the post, a dozen boys took most of the bands' horses two miles down the Yellowstone Valley. This was a fortunate move; otherwise they would have lost them.

The trading fort was enclosed by a tall fence of posts set side by side. In each corner rose a two-story log building overlooking the surrounding terrain. The fort could be entered by only one gate, which opened on the side toward the Crow camp. The gate was left open and no restrictions placed

on High Owl's people, for two different employees
of the post had Crow wives; also, Chicago's presence was a guarantee of good behavior.

About noon on the second day warning cries
were suddenly raised, and men of the War Club
Society, which served at that time as police of the
camp, began to arm themselves and run upstream.
A large body of Blackfoot warriors had crossed the
river. Crow men yelled, "To the fort! To the fort!"

Horse Tender had just mounted Spotted Pup,
ready to go hunting. She hastily rounded up the
two-dozen horses that grazed in the immediate vicinity and drove them into the center of camp. The
Crow defenders met the Blackfoot attackers and
slowed them with gunshots and yells. High Owl
called to them, "Don't sacrifice yourselves! Just
hold them up!" And to the women and children:
"To the fort! Take food and blankets! Let the
tepees stand! To the fort! Hurry! Take all weapons!"

The camp boiled with confusion for some swift
minutes. The Blackfoot raiders pressed forward deliberately. The Crow warriors retreated, only
trying to keep the enemy out of musket range of
their fleeing families and their hastily loaded
horses. The abandoned lodges were not in much
danger, being in gun range of the trading post.

When the last retreating Crows were in the compound and the large gate shut, the people relaxed
somewhat. Here and there a wound was examined,
cleaned, and bandaged. Many of the men peered
out cracks in the gate or climbed to a scaffolding
inside the palisade, or even to rooftops, in order to
see the terrain of the skirmish. Three Crow men lay
dead out there on the ground; in one of them a

spear stood up at an angle, its shaft decorated with
white feathers. The wives and kin of the slain, having looked about frantically, now realized the iden-
tity of the corpses they could see and set up a low
moaning and crying.

The field of the surprise engagement sloped
away unevenly to a point of trees a half mile distant. The ground had small ridges and shallow
gullies, and it bore low clumps of sagebrush. The
gaudy enemy warriors milled outside of musket
range, so that their shouts came indistinctly.

High Owl kept shouting, "Pay no attention to
them, the devils!"

The *bourgeois* shouted the same and added,
"They won't attack the fort!" The breeds of the
post and various Crow leaders agreed. The Blackfoot force outnumbered them all, but the palisade
walls more than evened the prospects.

They had not taken Horse Tender's suggestion
seriously when she asserted that she could speak
the enemies' language. Now she came riding her
spotted buffalo horse toward the gate, and they
stared aghast. She had a pistol in her waistband,
her bow and quiver on her back.

Antelope Man was seated propped against the
long wall of a building. He had sprained his bad
foot, and Birdy was rubbing it with bear fat. He
yelled, "Wait! Stop her! Wait! No, Horse Tender!"

The *bourgeois* and other men shouted: "What's
she doing? Stop that woman!" "The Blackfeet
don't want to talk!" "They will kill her!" "Close
the damned gate!" "You cannot talk to Blackfoot
devils!"

Mounted on the big paint, she seemed taller—no
feathers or other decorations, only the pistol and

bow and arrows. Perhaps it was because she rode so erect. Her hair was not braided, but gathered and tied with a thong behind her head, then trailing loose down her back. The crowd at the gate had to give way before her horse. She said, "Open the gate."

Perhaps she seemed even taller to those nearby on the ground, or perhaps it was something in her manner. In spite of continued shouted orders from leading men, the people swung wide the gate. She rode out.

Now a drama began to unfold before the eyes of the trading fort watchers, played out on a vast stage longer and wider than musket range. The Crows became quiet. She drew up a short way out of the walls, waiting for the enemy to see her. Five warriors gathered out of the distant ranks of Blackfeet and walked their horses forward. She kicked her spotted horse into a walk toward them.

It was a sunny day, of clear air. The scene stood out distinctly in its details. The watchers heard her cry out again and again to them in their foreign language. She must have been asking them what they wanted. The five fanned out as if to surround her. Then one raised a long gun to his cheek and fired; a puff of dirty smoke shot up and the report blasted the stillness.

But she had jerked young Spotted Pup sideways. She went off the horse as if she had kicked him away from her, landed running, bent low, and dropped behind a hummock of sage. They could see the short barrel of her pistol leveled, shining. When she fired, a Blackfoot warrior folded like a hit bird, then slumped headfirst off his horse. Now the watchers thought of her in a new way, for she had killed an armed enemy to justify her madness and to pay for her coming death.

The faint howls of the decorated Blackfoot warriors had anger in them. They fought their horses and spread even farther, to flank her on either side.

Her scared horse scampered back and forth behind her, its head flung to the side to avoid stepping on the trailing reins.

She did not stay in the concealment, but, ducking low, ran while she fitted an arrow to the bowstring. Though a low ridge hid her, the watchers held their breath, for she ran straight toward an enemy man. She rose suddenly, plain on the stage, and they could see her erect for a split instant, her long bow draw full. The enemy's startled horse threw him, and they could see as his limp body pitched up, the arrow shaft, front and back, through his chest.

The dim howls of the three remaining warriors seemed to have questions mixed with anger. Where is the enemy? How many are we fighting? They wheeled toward the center and began to retreat toward their lines, constantly looking to right and left.

She ran forward after them in the clear. Again the full-drawn bow was released. She screamed and her victim began a scream, which trailed off to silence as he hit the earth. The two remaining Blackfeet rode frantically toward their lines. She fell upon the downed warrior and pounded him again and again with her empty short gun, till she could retrieve her arrow out of him. She sprinted back to the other warrior shot with bow, and the watchers saw her pound at his brains with the pistol while she got her spent arrow. To her, obviously, the hitting was a practical matter; to the watchers it was more important. She had killed three enemies to pay for the three dead Crows, had taken their bows and quivers, also two muskets, had counted first, second, and third coup on two of them. This in plain view of most of the band.

As she caught her horse, the irregular line of Blackfeet surged toward her, but the Crows at the fort fired their muskets, and the enemy drew away.

When she rode back through the gate, her people were quiet, hardly believing what they had seen. She dismounted and lay the two captured bows and arrow cases and muskets before High Owl. She said, "They did not want to parley."

At this incongruous statement, they seemed released. They laughed and shouted war cries and some wept.

That night they could see the fires of the Blackfoot invaders. The Crows sent a continuous round of wolves down to their abandoned camp to make sure that their standing tepees and other property were not destroyed.

The Crows danced that night, not jubilantly, for they had lost lives, but they wanted their drum and singing to carry on the night air to their enemies. A blazing bonfire lighted the unfamiliar view of the compound and the log houses and the faces of Europeans and mixed blood among them.

The first song of many to be made about her did not even mention her name. It went thus:

> They do not want to parley.
> They do not want to parley.
> They want to sleep.
> They want to sleep.
> Sleep well, raiders of the Blackfeet.

Later, when the night was more than half spent
and their minds had become intent and their blood
was full of the drum sound, a famous old singer
made this song:

Revenge is sweet.
Now our dead can sleep.
What did our women do?
It is never seen,
But it is true.
We are going to see her darting form before us.
Now we see her rising up.
She is there.
What has Man Alone sent to the Crow Nation?

Those warriors absent on raids had returned
with their booty, and the frustrated Blackfoot
raiders had disappeared. High Owl had called a
council in the center of their camp in the edge of
the trees below the trading post.

The men of the council circle were aware of her
approach and were embarrassed. Another woman
or a child would have received a stern rebuke or at
least instructions to leave. They all became silent
and pretended to be thinking of weighty matters.
She came up behind Rainy, who sat next the chief,
and said, "Move over."

"What is it?" High Owl asked.

"I told Rainy to move and give me a place."

Most of them had yelled and sung themselves
hoarse celebrating her bravery a week before. Now
they seemed not so much angry as dumbfounded.

Finally the chief said, "Did you wish to speak to
the council? I believe we would hear you."

"No, I have decided to take my place in council."

A warrior at the other side said, "She should have sat with us for years. The stories about her are true."

Some family heads, seeing the drift of the matter began to frown and shake their heads. One heavyset man rose with some dignity, began to back away from the circle and said, "What is this? A woman? If this is a council, I may decide to leave."

"Go or stay as you please," she said, "I believe you are one of the men who drove me away from a buffalo surround years ago. If you ever raise a quirt to threaten me again, I'll put an arrow through your arm."

A second man rose and said, "Does a council mean nothing? I may leave myself."

"Go or stay as you please," she said. "Give my best wishes to your old parents. Two or three winters ago, when food was scarce, you had bad luck hunting, and I fed them elk meat for two moons."

Many eyes were on High Owl and Rainy. The latter had held the long-stemmed pipe when the council was interrupted. He had not passed it on, but puffed it absent-mindedly. He had withdrawn into his blanket so far that his face was hardly visible.

Here and there a man grunted, "Let her sit with us."

A third man, skinny and old, rose. He seemed angry, but tried to sound reasonable. "What is the world coming to? No one denies that the woman is the bravest woman we ever saw. And a good shot. We have sung her praises. Now, should we let her turn everything upside down? We are family heads and chiefs of soldier societies. Shall we let the women run the band?"

"She is not the women," someone said. "She is one person."

Apparently High Owl decided that it would be best to settle the question before the argument became more heated. "Please sit down," he said to the three standing. "I see no harm in her sitting with us and listening, at least for the present. Spread apart down there. Let her sit by Antelope Man."

Horse Tender said, "I asked Rainy to move over."

"Rainy? He sits on my right hand on purpose. If I am killed today, he will take my place tomorrow. Why do you want his seat?"

She said, "It would be an honor to sit between brave leaders."

"But you are embarrassing him. Why should he move over?"

"He will move when I tell you a story." They had somewhat spread apart the better to see her as she stood wrapped in a beautiful Navaho blanket, which she had borrowed from Birdy. "Four winters ago Rainy passed the pipe for a raid against a certain band of Lakota. He swore to kill the Lakota chief Streaked Hair. Rainy lost twenty-nine Crow warriors; he might have lost more, except for a kind of aid."

They murmured as they watched her: "The fourth wolf." *Napa* helped us." "I told you about her." "It was Old Man Coyote."

"Be quiet," the chief said.

She went on. "I see several men here who went on that raid. As you remember, a rumor went through the party and through the camp later."

"Are you the fourth wolf?" someone shouted.

"She is!"

"How could she be?"

"It was *Napa!* God's helper!"

"It was her! Horse Tender!"

"How could a woman do that?"

"She did it!"

"Now," she went on, "I ask that Rainy move over and give me a place. I have a gift to give him. I hold it now under my blanket."

Rainy found his tongue as all eyes were on him and the woman. "Thank you for the gift, but I don't need it. I've worried about the matter for four years, wondering what to say or do. I saw the fourth wolf that drizzling misty day when I thought I'd led all my men to death. The fourth wolf rode a black charger; it had the form of a human person and the breasts of a woman.

"I'm glad that Woman Chief has shown herself. As for the gift, I am guessing. No one has heard anything about Streaked Hair since that day."

She said, "I will let Rainy decide about the gift."

"Well, let us see it," he said. "The story has it that he wore two small copper bells pinned in his hair. Is that true, Woman Chief?"

He had called her Woman Chief twice and no one had seemed to notice. He had named her. Her friends would still call her Horse Tender, Chicago would call her Little Gal, See Dead Bull would call her Slave Girl; but from those moments when she stood straight as a pine outside the council circle, all eyes on her, she would bear the official name, the diplomatic name, the ceremonial name, of Woman Chief. White mountain men would come to call her Absaroka Amazon. Certain Crows would come to use a strange sort of underground name, Sweet Thunder Woman, but they would be persons of little consequence in the tribe.

. Now she said, "Excuse me," stepped to the center of the circle, drew from her blanket a scalp, and laid it with a small tinkle of copper bells on the ground before them. Then she stepped back.

They stared silently. It was a full scalp with two braids, shiny black except for a clear white streak as big as a finger from the front all the way down one braid. They looked at it and at each other during a long silence. She said, so softly that they had to strain to hear, "He was a stubborn enemy. He died hard. But he was not fast nor accurate with the bow."

In a minute Rainy said, "Well, move down there. Spread out a little and give me room to move. Make room. Make room. Woman Chief will get tired of standing up."

In the discussions that followed the council members found their voices. The main issue was that of moving safely to a new campsite, what place could be well defended, what area had good grazing, good hunting. Woman Chief did not assert herself above any other voice, but spoke briefly three times, then agreed to the consensus. At the close of the council, Rainy took the scalp to show to those band members who had lusted for revenge years before.

She had not solved all the problems of her role in the band, but had gained the sanction to have a voice, here and in the Crow Nation. Also, she now had the right to pass the pipe for raiding and war, the official privilege to ask whether men would follow her in dangerous pursuits.

12. Wealth

Ride Away had not been among the watchers that day at the trading fort, though he had heard it told, as they all had, many times. He became less comfortable with Horse Tender when they were out alone; he would remain quiet a long time, and when she prodded him into talking, would speak of some brave deed he hoped to do soon, not in specific but in general terms. When she passed the pipe for a raid east against the Cheyenne, he would not smoke, nor even talk to her about it.

They had made a successful fall meat hunt, but in the middle of it a small party of Cheyennes had struck the hunt camp, getting away with about a hundred first-class buffalo robes and a dozen horses. The Crows had not been able to pursue because of the need to continue the hunt and save the downed meat. Then High Owl planned to move west into the mountains for winter. There was no hope of recovering the stolen property, and the leaders were not in the mood for a mere harassing raid. They did not object if Woman Chief wished to do it.

She borrowed Antelope Man's stone pipe and offered it to select young warriors until six had accepted by taking a puff. Each had a muzzle-loading gun, long or short, among other weapons.

She said to Antelope Man, "Do not worry about me, Father."

"I have learned not to worry about you."

"If we are gone too long, you can trade a horse for some fresh meat. I promise to bring you some more horses before winter."

"All right."

She led her men out of camp after dark, beginning a strict discipline that they would come to hate and respect. When one of them wanted to wait till morning, she said, "How do you know there is not an enemy raiding party out there twice as strong as we are, waiting to watch and follow us?"

Though all six of the men had been on raids before, they had not been through such a regimen as now began. Always across open flat country they rode at night. In broken country, she would travel by day, but would lie for hours on her belly looking for bunches of buffalo or antelope; or watching eagles or hawks or vultures, to see whether they would light on some promontory ahead. Along streams, among the trees, she was willing to travel by day but kept two wolves out on the side hills ahead. They always moved on after building a cook fire, before sleeping.

They found that she would joke with them but would never let them forget who was the leader. One evening the one called Porcupine began to gather sagebrush for a fire. He had taken a small bundle wrapped in skunk hide out of his pack and placed it on a smooth rock.

"What are you doing?" Woman Chief asked.

"I'm going to open my medicine bundle. I have

to wash my hands and the bundle in sage smoke first."

"We're not going to build a fire here," she said. "We're going to sleep here."

"But it's powerful medicine," Porcupine insisted. "I bought it from One Good Eye. It will protect us and bring success."

"What's in it?"

"A magic rock and other things."

"Open it without the sage smoke."

"No! I'm not supposed to do that."

Woman Chief looked around at the terrain, then pointed. "You can go away over to the top of that hill and build a sagebrush fire if you want to. We're not going to build a fire here."

Porcupine looked surprised. "You don't want the help of strong medicine?"

She smiled at the four of them who were nearby, and they could not tell whether she was joking or serious when she said, "I have a strong secret medicine, which will bring success. It tells me that it's taboo to build a fire and sleep in the same place."

He put his medicine bundle back in his pack. They were all near the same age, but the men could not forget the songs about her. The following evening Porcupine tested her again. He said, "We have been talking. We think we're moving too slow."

She laughed. "I'm going to take all you boys home alive."

"But . . . well . . . what if the winter catches us in enemy country?"

"What's wrong with winter?" she asked. "Go slow and rest up, Porcupine. We may run day and night leaving enemy country."

"But . . . why do we go so slow?"

"I'm studying the country," she said. "I have secret medicine and also a vision. I saw many horses in a dream. I saw us dividing them up among us. If anyone had complained too much, he didn't get as many horses as the others."

Because she laughed about such matters, they did not know how to take her. They would say later that not even a rabbit or an owl knew when she passed through their country, but that she examined every rattlesnake and weasel and buzzard to see if they were allied with the enemy. She slept a little apart from the men, and they never knew when she rose to prowl the surrounding country.

The same day that the party came in sight of the dark, pine-studded slopes of the Black Hills they also located a Cheyenne camp. They watched it day and night for two days, the horse herds, the wood draggers, the women digging. The six men wanted to attack. Porcupine accused her of wanting to be too cautious, of planning too fully, of waiting and waiting, when what was needed was rash action. She said no and stared them down. When Porcupine pressed the matter, praising the virtue of boldness and quick action and surprise, she said, "Hold yourself ready to be bold, my friend, when the right time comes."

They turned north and made their way through the autumn countryside nearly as far as the Big River itself. She came into their sleeping area one morning at early dawn, woke them and said, "A Cheyenne band is moving toward their winter camp. Get up! Get ready! They feel safe. The camp has moved one day, but half of their horses are only now gathered and ready to follow today. It's only three boys and one old woman. Let them escape if they want to. We'll bring the horses over the pass down yonder, not up the valley."

Before the middle of the morning they had got into position and swooped down to cut off seventy Cheyenne horses. Two of the horse tenders were mounted, and Woman Chief deliberately pursued them on her paint warhorse until she was able to kill the mounts. The boys hid in the brush, as the other boy and old woman had done. The Cheyenne warriors would not learn about their loss this day.

She led the raiders and the captured horses up the shallow creek, staying in the water and on the rocky footing so that they left no tracks, then cut up over the low pass. They moved west at a trot through the afternoon, all night, till evening of the next day. Horses and riders were exhausted.

"I thought she would never stop," Porcupine said. "I'm grown to my horse. My legs will never work again."

They all got to laughing. As they gnawed at dried buffalo meat and watched their hobbled horses and the others grazing, she teased, "Do you think we should ride on tonight, Porcupine?"

He moaned and laughed at one time. They were all jubilant and could hardly believe how quickly they had struck and how successfully. She set no guard that night, but they slept in awed awareness that she prowled the surrounding high ground three different times in the darkness.

After seven days they slowed to allow the animals to take advantage of the good grazing in selected spots, and to kill and cook fresh game. She divided the horses among them, though they kept them in one herd. Each man got nine and she took sixteen, but there was no complaining.

The party entered the mountains and began to
search for the location of High Owl's camp, four of
them driving the horse herd and three fanned out
to high ground, looking. It was not a difficult
search, and one warrior soon reported its exact location. Horse Tender questioned him. Then they
crossed a low divide and she sent him in to inform
the band leaders that some Crow warriors were
coming home right away.

When he returned she questioned him about the
lay of the camp again, then gathered the six men
and gave them instructions. "Load your guns with
fresh powder and wadding. If you have some decorations to wear put them on. When we see the
camp I want the horses running. Fire in the air!
Fire! Keep yelling! Reload if you can, but keep the
horses running. I want to go right through the
middle of camp on the wide sand flat."

They moved up the valley. They sky was low,
and lazy snowflakes floated in the still air. They
melted in the creek water and on the bare ground,
but were beginning to build up on the evergreen
trees and on the drifts of dry leaves.

When they came in view of the lodges, steaming
under the gentle snow, they started their commotion, and Woman Chief led the thundering herd,
mounted on Spotted Pup. Smoke charged beside
her with his light pack, flinging his head and mane
as if he knew they were putting on a show. By the
time she was even with the first tepees, hundreds of
eyes were upon her. When the people saw the seventy running horses, they began to cheer.

High Owl's band danced late that night.

Woman Chief danced both with the warriors and with the women. When the drummers called the dance in which a woman is supposed to select a man for a partner, she searched among the watchers in the dim firelight and finally found Ride Away back at the edge of the crowd. The other men selected were following the women with big grins, but Ride Away looked solemn. He danced stiffly and in obvious discomfort.

That raid was a landmark in the development of the wealth of the lodge of Antelope Man. From that time there would be no worry about owning enough horses and property of all kinds. There would be horses and dried meat and skins to trade to other tribes, and robes and pelts to trade to Chicago and the trading posts, and always meat to give away and enough to make it a lodge known for hospitality.

It had become a two-tepee lodge. The master slept in one with his two wives. Woman Chief and Bad Woman and the mother-in-law, becoming slow and less talkative, slept in the other. Antelope Man's favorite occupation in good weather came to be to sit between his two tepees and invite some man to have a social smoke and drink a cup of coffee with sugar.

Now that she could hunt on an equal basis with men in the buffalo hunts supervised by soldier societies Horse Tender got all the robes they could handle. Each of the groups, the Foxes, the War Clubs, and the Big Dogs, argued the question as to whether she should be invited to join. Some members believed, without being able to give definite reasons, that she would be the cause of trouble in

their meetings and ceremonies and work. Wasn't it
enough that they honored her as a warrior chief?
Other members argued that if they did not invite
her, one of the other societies would get her. Finally, the Foxes asked her to join, and she politely
declined the honor.

To tan a first-class robe took many days of patient labor. Bad Woman proved her worth in this
as in other tasks. As had been promised, she was a
hard worker and productive, second only to See
Dead Bull. She came to be willing to show her face
not only to Horse Tender, but also to Birdy and
old Broken Ice.

One day Bad Woman had located a raft of dead
trees caught along the bank of the river. Horse
Tender brought two horses and began to help her
in the job of snaking the wood upstream and dragging it to the lodge. While they worked, they
talked.

"Are you happy with us?" Horse Tender asked.

"Yes. I'm the happiest in a long time."

"But, why?"

"Oh, I don't know. Because of work. I like to
work if people appreciate it. You have given me a
place to belong. You are the greatest, kindest . . ."

"Oh, shut up!" Horse Tender said. "Chop off
that big limb and quit talking like a slave."

They were knee-deep in water, trying to get the
wood loose. When Bad Woman became breathless
from chopping, she gave up the ax to her companion and continued the conversation. "When you
said you were the head of the lodge, I thought you
were crazy, but I was scared to kill myself. Then
when See Dead Bull was cross with me, I started to

run away, but you had told me to be patient and think about it and think again. I was amazed when I began to see that you were right."

"How can you be happy? Broken Ice still says bad things about you."

"A person should not get angry at very old people or young children."

"But See Dead Bull is still cross at you sometimes."

Bad Woman said, "That's enough chopping. I can pull and break it now." They were both wet and muddy to the waist. "See Dead Bull is a good worker. Some day she will teach me to be a tepee cutter."

"She used to beat me," Horse Tender said.

"But she doesn't now. I bet a fourth of the lodges in camp were cut by her. Wouldn't you be proud to do that?"

"I'm glad you like her," Horse Tender said. "Let's leave those small limbs that are caught in the brush. We are going to have a lot of wood. We'll be giving away wood to lazy people."

They slogged along the shallows, guiding the horses and pushing on the tangle of driftwood. The horses pulled awkwardly against the ropes low on their necks, stumbling in the muddy footing. When they stopped to rest, Horse Tender asked, "Didn't you ever want to have a baby?"

Bad Woman said, "If I could have it without a man." They both laughed.

"Do you hate all men?"

"No. I like Antelope Man, but I don't want to be his wife. I like men all right."

"There's a man in camp who lives with his brother. His name is Little Wolf. He's partly blind.

He's old, but not too old. And not too bad-looking. He's not married. He can see a fire or a tepee, but not a person's face."

Bad Woman had begun to laugh.

"I'm serious," Horse Tender said. "I could tell Antelope Man to have him come visit, and you could serve him coffee."

Bad Woman kept laughing and said, "I'll tell you what would be even better. You could get me a young handsome one and you could put out his eyes so he couldn't see me."

They both laughed. But later when they were even with the camp and were struggling to get the crooked wood out of the water, Horse Tender said, "I'm serious about one thing."

"What?"

"If you ever had a baby and gave it to me, I would pay you whatever you asked. I would get you jewelry and the best dresses a woman ever had or whatever you wanted. You could nurse it, but it would be mine."

Bad Woman looked at her a moment and did not laugh.

Her relationship with Ride Away continued to lose some of the spontaneity and delight that it had held when they were younger. He would not stay with her in some private retreat more than one short night and would not play foolishly. When they argued, she had to be the one to bring them back together. Finally it came to the point that he obviously avoided her. Whereas they once had been able to read each other's mind and know where the other would be, now he was never there.

Horse Tender deliberately followed him one day,

dismounted where he sat on a dead log, and stood in front of him some minutes. She finally said, "Please don't turn against me."

"I'm as brave as you are," Ride Away said.

"I know you are. Please don't turn against me. I need you. You are probably braver."

"You don't really think so. You need somebody? They sing your name! They put you with the greatest warriors of the past, and with the legends. When I first saw you, I thought you were just a girl and I was just a boy."

"Please don't turn against me, Ride Away. I love you."

"You have ruined my life," he said. "And every great thing you do, you make it more impossible for us. And I can't even get interested in another woman now, after knowing you. How can I sleep with a legend! You're not a girl anymore; you're a legend and a song!"

"But wait! I don't mean to be! Look at my arm! I'm not half as strong as you, nor half as brave!"

His face was full of anguish. "Be kind to me," he said. "Great mother woman, lie to your little boy to make him feel good. You can see an arrow go around in flight, and know how far the wind will push it to the side. Why don't we have a shooting contest? You are so accurate that you could always miss and let me win and feel proud."

"Ride Away, please don't! What can I say? It's the way you're thinking. I didn't make it this way. It's the way people have been thinking in the past. That's the trouble. It's not me!"

"No, it's not you! Why don't you pet me on the head?"

"Please don't, Ride Away! Chicago: I believe

what he said. It's just friends and babies and children. Working with people and for people you want to be with. Talking to them. Doing your best for them, and them doing their best for you. That's enough for anybody. Even the big King of England, Chicago said, or the president of the whites, that's all a human person needs. I don't want any more than that."

"Horse Tender," he said. "I mean Woman Chief. You think I'm stupid. I'm not so quick-witted as you, but I'm not stupid. If all women were like you, then things would be different, and men would have to accept it. It would be all right. It would work. But you are not a woman; you're a legend and a song. You say 'babies.' Where is my son for me to teach and my daughter for me to protect? Half-grown boys, and girls too. They worship a father and hang on his words. Where are they for me? You have left me standing on the prairie alone without food or water or children or friends. Listen, Woman Chief, you are a Crow thing like Tobacco Planting. I'm only a man. You have ruined my life. I have to leave you and stay away from you. You are like the cruel white winter that comes from the north. I speak to you from the bottom of my heart. You are a Crow thing like Tobacco Planting."

She reached out her hand toward his shoulder, and he stepped back. She said softly, "I'm not a Crow, Ride Away."

"What?"

"I'm not a Crow. I'm an Atsina. I'm a human being and a woman."

"You're one of the three or four best-known Crows in this whole land!"

"I'm not even a Crow. Don't you think I remember my Atsina mother and father? I wouldn't want Antelope Man to know, but I think about them. I remember the day my first mother took me off the cradle board and I was free to run around. I couldn't talk well, but I tried to tell them something about the cradle board, and my first father understood and told my mother to burn up the board. So she did. She put it on the fire. They laughed at me, and I laughed and danced.

"Ride Away, I was never anything but a human being. After they died of smallpox, we were camping with a Blackfoot band, and I tried to follow a Blackfoot man and woman who had a little girl my age, but they wouldn't take me. Finally, I found me a father and I took See Dead Bull for a mother, even though she doesn't know it.

"Ride Away, if you will just give me two more years to get horses and robes, I'll come to your lodge and drag wood and cook and make your clothes and obey every order you tell me. Give me two years and I'll never ride a horse or pull a bow again in my life."

He laughed in a strained way. "You know why that's funny? One time you asked me wouldn't it be funny if a coward who was a good marksman killed a brave man who shot crooked? Well, wouldn't it be funny if a family starved to death for meat while the greatest hunter in the world did woman's work in the lodge? I've given you more than two years, Woman Chief."

"You don't have to call me that!"

"No, but I have to look at the truth. I can see our lodge. I can see the council men come and tell me and the children to get out, because they want to consult with Woman Chief."

"We could move to another band."

"The whole Crow Nation knows you. Even the enemies all around know you. I'm glad I knew you. Can you understand that? I figured out from my training those important things: bravery and medicine and telling the truth in council. I have the bravery; don't you dare think I don't! But I met you. I learned how to be a good Crow man, but I met you. I could have been an honored warrior, but I met you. I was stupid. I'm glad now that I knew you, but I didn't know the price. I guess I would do it all over again, but I'm looking at the truth today. You have left me on the bare prairie and every direction I look is nothing but dirt and sagebrush and cactus and dry distance."

She said softly, "It's not my fault."

"No, of course it's not! I'm glad you said you're not a Crow."

"But I really am."

"No, you're not. I'm a Crow. You are not even an Atsina. You may be greater than both of them. I don't know what you are."

"Can't we just be a man and woman?"

"No. This tribe says what a man is and what a woman is."

"Do you want me to get down on my knees and beg you?"

"No."

She suddenly tensed with anger. "I'm not going to beg you anymore."

"I hope you don't. It's painful to me. But some day I will show you something about me; then you will remember my words."

"Right now you are showing me how to be jealous and petty! I said that I love you and it doesn't mean anything to you!"

"When I show you," he said, "maybe you will understand."

She strode away from him as if there would never be another word spoken between them, but when she had gone a short way, he yelled, "Wait!" She slowed and stopped and waited, without looking at him.

In a minute he came to her. "I think I should tell you what I have to do. I'm . . . well, I'm going to lead a raid. I have to capture some horses."

She did not look at him, but asked, "Where will you go?"

"It's not planned yet. Only in my mind. I want only a half dozen young warriors. It will be successful. I need to get at least ten horses for myself if possible."

"Ride Away, I can give you, or I mean make Antelope Man give you, ten horses."

His voice hardened again. "You have not understood a thing I've said."

"No, I have not. Why did you say 'wait'? You don't need my permission to plan a raid."

"I don't need your permission to marry either, but it seems right to let you know."

"What do you mean?"

"I have pressure on me from my family. They want to know why I'm not married at my age. There is this girl. Her grandfather used to be a great warrior and he fought beside my grandfather."

"So you need horses to purchase her."

"I need horses for all the reasons anyone else needs horses."

"So you mean to live your life by what your family wants."

"Why shouldn't I be married? I find myself always with the unmarried men and boys, all of them younger than me."

"Who is this expensive woman?"

"A girl they call Little Rose."

"That bitch!"

"You have no right to call her that."

"She's cheap and stupid and silly and her family is a bunch of nobodies with no pride and no wealth and nothing else."

They stood in silence for a long minute, then he finally said, "Horse Tender, I don't need your permission to marry, but I want . . . well . . . I really want you to agree that things will never work for you and me. I want you to understand. And agree. I mean . . . please. Do you understand?"

They stood in silence again, for an interminable period, before she walked away. He remembered the time after the old black mare was eaten by wolves, and she had beaten the wolf to death with a club, and he had thought, in the midst of her unreasoning anger, that she had tears on her cheeks.

13. Council Woman

When Little Smoke was two years old he was as big
as his sire, was equally rebellious against anybody
other than his mistress, and had boundless energy.
He was beginning to compete with Old Smoke and
with his half brother, Spotted Pup. If Horse Tender
rode one, the other two tried to go along and outrun the one that was mounted. The three fought
over which should be the leader of Antelope Man's
growing herd of mares and geldings, but did not
push their aggression beyond a few bites and small
hoof cuts, lest they offend the human female who
dominated them. Apparently the three stallions
had the ambition of breeding all the mares belonging to High Owl's band, and they did more than
their share.

In the year after the seventy-horse raid Woman
Chief led two more. She had no trouble getting
warriors to accompany her, but rather had to pass
the pipe secretly and slip out of camp with her party. She struck first against a Blackfoot-Atsina
camp up beyond the Musselshell, where she took a
reasonable number of horses and booty. With only
a fortnight's rest, she went south all the way to the
Platte against an unguarded Arapaho camp. Her

warriors took the camp and six scalps and paid one life and several wounds. The men said that she was a thoughtful tactician, that she had magic in her bow or in a musket, that she had no trace of fear.

After the first welcome back from the south, she brought her share of the plunder, packed on three *mulos*, to the lodge of Antelope Man. The *mulos* were animals from the Spanish, much like horses except harder working, more docile; they had longer ears and did not breed. Antelope Man exclaimed, "We're rich! Let's see what you've got! Open the packs!"

Birdy was almost like a child, expecting unheard of gifts. "Hurry, Horse Tender! Be generous!"

She did not look like a war chief nor act like one as she stood in the fluttering shade of a giant cottonwood tree in the presence of the three strange pack animals, one man, four women. "Father," she said. "It's not . . . well . . ." It was the first time she had ever called him father in the presence of his first wife.

"What I mean . . . well . . . it's mostly not for a man. I thought you could have the three *mulos* and a bag of tobacco. But could someone else divide the rest?"

They stared at her, not understanding. Old Broken Ice crouched in the door of the second tepee, watching; she could not walk anymore and talked little. Bad Woman, with her small cloth tied across her face, waited to be told how she should help. Birdy looked at her husband. See Dead Bull stood as silent and enigmatic as a sandstone cliff.

Antelope Man limped between the pack beasts, pulling at the knots that tied the bulging packs. He said, "We agree. We will take whatever you say,

Horse Tender. Don't keep us waiting so long."

"But, Father, could the first woman of the lodge
do it? It seems proper. She is in charge of certain
things."

He asked, "What? See Dead Bull?"

"Yes, it seems proper."

"But she must take what you give her like the
rest of us do."

Horse Tender said, "I give it all to her and she
can divide it up."

Antelope Man laughed and said to his first wife,
"You heard her! Divide it up!"

See Dead Bull frowned and shook her head.

"I order you to do it," he said.

She soon had the other women helping her to get
the packs untied and opened on the ground. They
exclaimed over the new property: trade goods,
food, cloth, items made by hand. There were
twelve Navaho blankets, red and orange and
brown and yellow; jewelry of smooth blue stones
and white metal; cooking utensils; a Spanish saddle
with varicolored leather and metal ornaments.

See Dead Bull became thoroughly embarrassed.
She appealed to Antelope Man: "I can't do it."

"Why not?"

"I don't know what to do. I would give some to
my family here and some to my friends and some
cooking pots and cloth to some poor people."

"I order you to do it," he said. "You are the first
woman of this lodge. Take what you like best and
divide some and give some to friends and poor people."

"I don't know . . ."

Horse Tender said, "Maybe she wants to wait
and not do it right now. We can store it."

"Yes! Yes, I have to wait and think," See Dead Bull said.

It was several days before the first wife got all the property distributed. She finally brought the saddle and two blankets and a necklace and laid them in front of Horse Tender, who said, "Thank you."

The first wife stood there as if she wanted to say something and did not have the words. Finally she said, "I hope it's all right, the way I have divided things."

"It's fine. Thank you very much."

"You are welcome, Horse Tender." It was the first time the woman had used the name Horse Tender, and it meant that there was peace between them, but the older woman was not ready to call her daughter.

The incongruity of her position as a leader of warriors caused many Crows to exaggerate her feats and assign magic to her that she had not demonstrated. At a dance one night a singer made this song about her:

> Hear her war cry on the prairie.
> Let's go where the fight is thickest.
> Hear her yell down in the valley.
> Hurry where the fight is thickest.
> Hear her wild scream on the mountain.
> Let's go where the fight is thickest.
> Hear our Woman Chief pursuing.
> She is a Crow person.

It appeared that her position on the council was strong, for she spoke whenever she chose and the men paid attention. It was the custom to get unanimous consent to decisions; the minority had the right to long discussion, but failing to convince enough others, it would yield. And not merely to the will of the majority, but to its wisdom; however; the majority was not defined only by numbers, rather by depth of feeling and commitment and character.

It was not clear whom Woman Chief represented. Other council members were heads of families or soldier societies. Sometimes she spoke as if her mind were on the Crow Nation as a whole; she believed that the Blackfoot peoples to the north and the Sioux peoples to the east and southeast would destroy them and overrun their land if they did not give back raid for raid and attack for attack. She believed that they should camp and hunt north of the Musselshell and east in the valley of the Powder, several bands near each other if possible, thus asserting their determination to retreat no farther.

Perhaps the most original proposal made by Woman Chief was one that was designed to give recognition to two selected women each year when the Sun Dance was held. In this council meeting there had not been much business to discuss, and the circle sat silent for some minutes. When the pipe came to her, she held it instead of passing it on. She introduced her subject casually.

Some man said, "We already honor women at the Sun Dance and at the Tobacco Planting."

"We honor them for chastity," she said. "That is good. A pure and virtuous girl or woman is valuable. But if all our women just sat still and remained chaste, we would starve and freeze and have no beauty in our lives."

Here and there around the circle the men grunted. She went on: "We could choose one woman who is a good cook and always has plenty of food stored and plenty of firewood and keeps a friendly lodge and is hospitable. Then we could choose one woman who makes beautiful dresses and moccasins and new bead designs and plaited horsehair bridles and decorated cradle boards and painted skins."

Some man asked, "Who would do the choosing?"

"Maybe the women. Maybe High Owl would tell his wife and two other important women to think about a way to let all the women choose. Then in those years when we have a Sun Dance, let the crier announce: 'High Owl's band has chosen so-and-so to be our Good-Lodge-Woman this year,' and let the drummer beat softly, and let her walk between the rows of people and cut a bite of the buffalo tongue that hangs on the sacred pole, then pass back between the lines of people. And let the crier say: 'High Owl's band has chosen so-and-so to be our Beautiful-Handwork-Woman this year,' and let her parade the same."

In a moment Elk Head commented: "It will cause jealousy among the women."

"Perhaps not if they do the choosing. If one deserves it, some year her turn will come."

Apparently they found it a novel idea and were not against it, but merely dubious.

Finally High Owl said, "Our ceremonies are ancient and handed down by our ancestors. Ceremonies have a sacred nature about them."

"They were made by wise council members long ago," she said. "They have become sacred by use.

What if we did this thing, then the other Crow
bands took it up and at Sun Dance they each presented their Good-Lodge-Woman and Beautiful-
Handwork-Woman? Then people would say that
the wise council of High Owl's band made this ceremony for the Crow Nation."

They seemed to like the idea that they might ori-
ginate a custom that would be extended and preserved. "We could try it," one said, "and see if other Crow bands pick it up." Another said, "Let's try
it."

Woman Chief went on: "Perhaps sooner or later
this council would decide to invite those two wom-
en to sit with us. They probably would not speak
much, but they would listen and would be ready to
state their ideas."

After some pondering, High Owl said, "We
speak for our women. Many men listen to their
women in private."

"I don't suggest we do this now," she said. "But
I say we might. Good women are half the tribe. If
this wise council decided to seat women, they
might speak some ideas that they don't tell their
husbands."

She had almost gone too far. After some com-
ments around the circle, a consensus seemed to de-
velop that they should honor two women at the
coming Sun Dance. The method of selecting them
was not clearly established.

Woman Chief was not a diplomat. In the following weeks a flurry of excitement ran through the
women of the band. Then jealousy reared its petty
head, and some women like Antelope Man's first
wife ignored the proposal altogether. The two
women chosen were compromises, would offend

no one, and everyone knew that they were not the
Best-Lodge-Woman and the Most-Beautiful-
Handwork-Woman. Finally, at the Sun Dance
gathering the other Crow bands sensed the compromises when the two honorees were announced
and they were not impressed.

Ironically, while they would not follow her ideas
for improving the lot of women, the assembled
Crows talked of Woman Chief herself endlessly.
One singer made this song:

> They cannot stand against her.
> She kisses each arrow, her lips
> As red as new blood.
> Time is little enough at best, oh stranger!
> Stop your way and come with us to the river.
> Drink your fill in our woman's fast river.

And when they danced late one night another
singer made this:

> Come and see our Woman Chief, Lakota!
> You sing it is a good day to die.
> Come on! Make her acquaintance to yourself.
> No man lives forever, oh brave enemy Lakota.
> Come and try to take our lands
> And meet our Woman Chief.

Ride Away had traveled east two days with his
raiding party of five young warriors when he found
that he was being followed. It was afternoon and
he had to squint against the sun to see the moving
black speck behind them on the rolling prairie. The
wind stirred the tan autumn grass in the distance
and made seeing difficult, but the tiny black figure

became a mounted horse coming in a pacing gait. Just before sundown Ride Away pointed out to his men a camping spot ahead, then turned back to investigate.

It was Horse Tender. He rode straight toward her and she did not try to conceal herself.

He rode up and blocked her way and said angrily, "I don't like this! What do you think you're doing? You can't stick your nose into my business this way!"

She dismounted patiently. Her bow case and quiver were slung on her back, and her hair blew loose in the wind. When he had dismounted, she said, "I don't mean to interfere. But you said something the last time we talked . . ."

"There won't be any fourth wolf on this raid," he said. "I know what I'm doing and I don't need any help from you or from anybody else."

"You said you would do something to show me; then I would understand."

"I will. There won't be any fourth wolf on my raid to help me. I don't want you here."

"Ride Away, I'm not here to help you or to interfere at all. But you said you would do something to show me. Like it was a brave and daring thing. I want to ask you not to do some foolish thing. Please. Not for me. I admire you. Please don't take risks you don't have to. Not for me. If you got hurt, I would feel like it's my fault. Please, Ride Away."

He said, "If I do something brave, is that foolish? What do you think it does to my reputation with my warriors to have a woman following me?"

"I'll go back, but I have something else to say."

The sun had set behind a low cloud bank, and the western sky was brilliant red and pink. Their two horses, instead of cropping grass, stood as if listening to their conversation. She went on: "You said you don't need my permission to marry that girl. You don't. But . . . I know you don't. But . . . well, I give you my permission, but please don't do it. I understand, Ride Away, but please don't do it."

"We've talked everything over a hundred times," he said. "I will never talk to you again until I show you something."

"I do understand, Ride Away."

"Are you going to leave?"

"Yes."

They waited a minute under the brilliant sky, then mounted their horses. As they rode in opposite directions each looked back at the other.

It was about this time that the strange, sort of underground name, Sweet Thunder Woman, became established. It would come to be used by the few *berdaches,* those unmanly but thoughtful men, by some elderly men and women, by some children who did not quite fit into tribal life. The logic of the name was uncertain. She was not afraid of thunderstorms, and rumor said that she sometimes prayed to Thunder. Then there was the idea that Thunder need not always be feared, if he stayed at a distance and sent a shower onto the hot ground and left the air smelling sweet.

Then there was probably confusion with Sweet Grass Woman, a legendary person hardly even remembered by the storytellers. A certain grass was called sweet grass because grazing animals preferred it and it smelled good when burned. Some unusual woman had evidently been named after it in the ancient past, and Woman Chief was confused with her.

But then it could have been only that the *berdaches* and other misfits wanted a private name for her. That they saw the contrast in the words Sweet and Thunder and sensed a fitness in the name. That because she was generous in giving meat where it was truly needed without being ostentatious and because they saw, or thought they saw, that she had a frustrated tenderness, they wanted to put the good name of Sweet to qualify the fearful name of Thunder. In any case, it was only persons of little consequence who called her Sweet Thunder Woman.

14. The Revenge of Ride Away

Broken Ice died in the winter time. Too proud to be an invalid, as Pea Finder had been, she threw herself away by dragging herself out of camp one snowy night. They found her frozen the next morning. The four remaining women and one man of Antelope Man's lodge missed her, for she had been a presence, though she had not used her caustic tongue in a long time. She had left a valuable gift, her knowledge of tepee cutting, to her eldest daughter, See Dead Bull.

The lodge now had in it the two most competent and hard-working women in the band in the persons of Bad Woman and See Dead Bull. It had the most successful hunter and raider. In Birdy it had a fair worker. In Antelope Man it had a man who truly enjoyed their wealth, for he loved to invite a guest for a smoke or coffee or a meal, and he took pride in being able to give modest presents. If something was lacking in the lodge, it was subtle, hard to put one's finger on.

Chicago, perhaps more thoughtful than Antelope Man, wondered about the woman chief, whom he called Little Gal. She seemed changed. Was it only maturity? That she had lost girlishness?

187

She was friendly and still liked lighthearted banter, but sometimes for a moment a cast of solemnity, almost sorrow, came into her face.

The band had moved west up a fork of Greybull River. High Owl had come to strongly prefer the mountain valleys during the heat of the summer. They climbed north over the rough hills and canyons to the headwaters of the Stinking Water and found a campsite only a two-day's ride from that basin where hot water and steam and an evil smell shoot up out of the earth. Plenty of deer and elk could be found. The streams were icy even in hottest weather and they could see the snow of the Absaroka Peaks.

But their scouts and hunters soon brought startling news. The rough land to the north was crawling with Blackfeet.

This was clearly Crow country, but the enemy warriors did not seem disposed to flee. During the next several days Crow scouts encountered three or four bunches of Blackfoot men, totaling no more than sixty, and they did not have any women with them or a settled campsite. It was a raiding party, looking for an opportunity. The encounters caused little damage on either side, for an outnumbered group could quickly find a defensive position.

For some days High Owl's band played a dangerous game with them. The necessary tactics were twofold: that scouts range widely in order to know how many enemy were in the vicinity and that every precaution be taken against surprise. Any tactic such as flanking or surrounding, which might have worked on the plains, was impractical, for much of the terrain consisted of steep slopes where horses could not go, and even sheer cliffs where warriors could not go. The Blackfeet seemed to understand the situation as well as did the leaders of High Owl's people.

One day about the middle of the morning the enemy appeared, evidently the entire group, on a ridge shaped like a saddle less than a mile from camp. The Crows were on Eagle Nest Creek and the saddle made a natural pass over to the neighboring valley. Most of the Crow warriors, except for the War Clubs, who were on scouting and guard duty, rode out to face the enemy.

Neither side could advance without heavy losses. The Blackfeet, highly decorated with feathers, waited near the top of the pass, where large boulders would give protection. A small patch of thick pines would even hide their horses. One of them rode forward, shouting insults and shaking his fist. He came into long musket range and drew up.

Two Crow arrows fell short, though they had been arched high in the air. Three Crow marksmen tried their muskets and raised spits of dust near him, but the lone Blackfoot sat calmly and eyed them with contempt.

"He's a good judge of gun range," Woman Chief said.

Mounted on the big stallion Little Smoke, she was talking with High Owl, Rainy, and Elk Head. They had decided that there was no way to dislodge the enemy and at the same time protect the camp.

Elk Head asked her, "What are they shouting?"

"Only foolishness," she said. "It's my guess that they are about to leave our country and are just shouting a few insults before they go."

When the enemy warrior had ridden back up the slope, a Crow warrior rode forward in a walk, shouting, "Blackfoot cowards! You cannot shoot! Dogs! Old women! Babies! You cannot shoot!" He pulled up within long musket range and gave the same demonstration of bravery as had the enemy warrior.

After three Blackfeet and two Crows had performed the feat, all of them unscathed, Ride Away, the grandson of old One Good Eye, rode forward. He went slightly farther than the others, dismounted, and seated himself on a rock that stood up waist high. One enemy bullet careened off the rock, but he did not move. After a minute, he remounted his horse.

But he did not turn back. He raised his war club, screamed, and charged.

It was surprising how far he got. The enemy had expected no such act, and only two or three had weapons at the ready. Among the Crow gathering, warriors gasped at first, then some began to cheer. A woman's voice rose among the Crow leaders: "Oh, no! Please don't! Turn back! Turn back! Oh, no!" They saw Ride Away's horse stagger, saw him beat the beast forward, saw Ride Away jerk, then regain his seat. Finally the horse went down, and the Crow warrior walked on up the incline, wavering from side to side, his war club raised. He was only ten steps from the nearest Blackfoot when he fell flat. The enemy swarmed over him.

The leading war chief of the Crow Nation was crying like an Indian woman.

The Crow warriors moved forward, but the Blackfeet retreated over the saddle pass and disap-

peared. Apparently they were satisfied to take one
scalp and go back to their own country.

Chicago was worried about her. He had guessed
years before the relationship between Woman
Chief and the young warrior Ride Away. Now she
was not able to claim the body or help in the scaffold burial, for he had many respectable relatives
and had recently joined the Fox Society; thus many
men and women had the right to help honor the
warrior who had shown such bravery. Chicago saw
Horse Tender with her self-inflicted wounds, her
arms slashed and dripping blood, standing back
alone as if she did not belong anywhere.

They built a scaffold of lodgepole pines on a
knoll within walking distance of camp and thereon
placed the body, wrapped in bright blankets and
tied securely. They put presents inside the wrappings and outside, even tied them to the scaffold,
which was as high as a tall man can reach. Women
cried and moaned. Chicago saw that Little Gal,
self-wounded, stood back in the trees and watched.

He was aware that she had not come back into
camp that night. As he was hunting for her, he returned to the knoll where the scaffold stood and
found a strange addition. Tied to the posts by
ropes about their necks were two dead horses,
sprawled on the grass, wide-eyed, stiff, their
throats cut. They were the old stallion Smoke and
the stallion late in his prime, Spotted Pup, both
war-horses and great hunters.

It is said by the Crow people and by the allies
and strange people that in the next uncertain world
where persons go, they will be beautiful and strong.
That the women will not be infirm or pitiable, but

if they were adept diggers of *pomme blanc* or fin-
ders of prairie pea caches or if they were skilled
tepee cutters, then they shall be at their best there.
They will be desirable and full of laughter and
women's wisdom. And men will not be weak,
though they die old; they will have the manhood
beauty and bravery of twenty-five winters. Therefore, it seems possible that horses are the same, for
there shall certainly be horses in the next world to
let men take their feet out of the dirt and to let
them ride and range broadly over the heavenly
plains. Also, it seems possible that a bloody, weeping woman, who was their god, explained to and
instructed the stallions that though they had never
let him ride, they must now be Ride Away's great
war-horses and racers and hunters.

Chicago hunted for her three days and was
aware that Antelope Man was also limping
through the canyons and wading ice-cold streams
and climbing rocks, looking for her. Chicago
found her in a kind of grotto under a bluff, sitting
on a whitened drift log. He ran, puffing through his
whiskers, back to camp and found Antelope Man.
The two came back to her at midday, and she was
still sitting in the same attitude on the log with her
face buried in her hands.

Her arms had bled down onto her hands and
clothing, and, according to the custom of grieving
women, she had opened the wounds anew each
day. The two men went up to her. Antelope Man
said softly, "Daughter, are you asleep?"

Then a moment later: "Daughter, are you
awake?"

She raised her head. The blood on her hands had
not been dry and it had painted her face in

grotesque patterns. As she looked at them and spoke, her face became contorted and ugly. "What am I going to do?"

Antelope Man said, "You are coming home. I'm the head of the lodge and it's time for you to obey some orders from me. You will come home and eat and rest, and I will wash your face and arms with warm water and take care of you."

It was a week later that she walked into a council meeting, which had been discussing a location for a winter camp. They became silent and waited for her to sit down, but she did not. If anyone expected an explanation of her behavior during the past few days, he was disappointed.

She asked abruptly, "Who has passed the pipe for revenge?"

They looked from one to the other and High Owl said, "No one, as yet."

"They come into our land," she said, "and kill our best men. I want thirty warriors, as many as we can safely spare, experienced men who can ride and scout and fight without resting. I want men who are not so much interested in booty as in dead enemies."

High Owl asked, "How will you know what division of the Blackfeet to strike?"

"I'm going against all the Blackfoot Nation," she said, "and their trashy allies the Big Belly Atsinas, and against all the Lakota and Cheyenne and their running dogs, the Arapahoes."

"Will you do it with thirty warriors?"

"I can do it with thirty fast and tough warriors, but men from other Crow bands will join me. I mean to make our enemies back away. Will your

children and their children and their children have
a homeland? Will they have hunting grounds? Or
even life?"

She seemed hard and brittle and uncompromis-
ing. They could see the scars on her arms where
they extended outside her blanket. Some of the
council members were almost afraid of her.

"Do not be mistaken," she said, "about what it
means for those who ride with me. They will be
tested harder than ever before. They will see danger
and hardship. I don't want any babies! I want what
you consider men! And I will make you more than
men! I will make you what Crow people should
be."

She became passionate, towering in front of
them. Perhaps the songs about her had gone to her
head or perhaps her desire for revenge made her
seek a covering explanation for her feelings. "I
have no children! Why? Because I am sent to be
your mother! Your mother! You have two mothers
and I am one! All your children are my grandchildren! Will they have a homeland? Will they
possess these mountains and plains? Or will the
cowards who surround us prevail and the Crow
Nation disappear like mist under the sun?"

She lowered her voice, but it was still hard. "Do
not volunteer to go with me if you are afraid."

High Owl was three times her age, yet he stared,
half believing, at the idea that she was his mother.
Those around the council circle who disagreed with
her were confused or reluctant to argue.

Elk Head said, "I will go with you. And
persuade some other men."

"We need to select rather than to persuade," she
said.

The irony of the fact that he who had led the raid long ago when she was taken as a child now agreed to follow her seemed to go unnoticed. During the remainder of the council and during the two days of preparation, it was understood that Elk Head would be her second in command.

She was even more strict than she had been before. She examined the weapons and equipment of all the young warriors who wanted to accompany her and made scathing remarks about anything that she did not deem adequate. She rejected half of the arrows one warrior intended to take and told him fiercely, "Never shoot a crooked arrow at an enemy! It will only make him angry!"

To those of the thirty who did not own two good war-horses, she gave from Antelope Man's large herd, and even insisted, successfully, that High Owl, Rainy, and One Good Eye contribute their best mounts.

The oldest among the Crows remembered from their grandparents stories how *Maga-hawathus* had sent the horse to the plains people, how at first it had been called Big Dog or Seven Dogs, because it was a much better servant to human beings than the dog, and how some of the Snake Indians had called it God Dog, because it was so much more than a beast of burden. And during those generations, when the people learned to range widely and ride like lords over the broad body of the earth, no one had ever seen such a swift, effective, cruel striking force as now followed Woman Chief.

The men would say that they had thought they knew about war, but found that they had never understood how long and far and fast men could ride, how complete scouting could be, how only thirty could sweep through two different enemy villages in one day, destroying their property and killing their most stubborn defenders. Elk Head was amazed at the accuracy of her tactics. She would say, "Take ten men and circle into the willow brakes. The first enemy who run out will try to hide below the bank in front of you. When you have killed as many as you can, ride up the streambed to meet me. The main body will try to protect their horse herd." And it would turn out nearly exactly as she had said.

Neither Elk Head nor any of the men found reason to criticize her leadership. Quite the opposite. They each hoped not to shame himself in front of her. There were times for patient scouting, secrecy, long weary rides through the night; but also times for audacious boldness. She knew somehow when the time had come to charge. Then, no one of the thirty, though he whip his horse unmercifully, could come up even with their leader on her mount Little Smoke.

She brought her party back from the first bloody tour to the north—the twenty-eight who still lived out of thirty—while the leaves were falling and after High Owl's band had already settled into winter camp. They brought seventeen enemy scalps. She immediately announced that they would only rest five days, then ride north again, and would not be dissuaded by the threat of coming winter. Though all the twenty-eight wanted to go with her again, she rejected half of them and replaced them with other men who were fresher or might be better fighters. Half the horses were also replaced.

The second foray was as successful as the first,

except that she led them farther. They roamed like a pack of wolves whose hunger is insatiable against the exposed and unsuspecting victims in their winter villages. Her raiding followers knew that she led them dangerously far north, but they followed her anyway, and the icy fingers of white winter softened their grasp enough to let her pass through with her vengeance—as if white winter itself were not implacable, but were willing that she have her way. And even in those cold lands that some white man had called *Alberta* and *Saskatchewan* they found cured grass with the snow blown off and also cottonwood bark to sustain their mounts, and they took replacement horses and pemmican from the hated Blackfeet and their stinking allies, while those people scattered in the bloody snow.

Coming south they paused in the Bearpaw Mountains. The weather was good, as if winter looked elsewhere and gave a reprieve. The land was colored gray. The only snow lay in drifts against the shadowed banks of dry gullies. The mountains rose out of the plains in peaks and knolls and bluffs, and the courses of small creeks were marked by the dark, leafless tangle of trees and brush. They kept scouts moving always in every direction.

It was late afternoon when a young warrior named Skyboy, greatly distracted, came to the fire where some twenty of the raiders warmed their hands.

"What's the matter with you?" someone asked.

His eyes were wide as if with fear and surprise as he looked at them. He had just come down from a nearby knoll. "She hit me on the face with her hand!" he said.

"What?"

"What did he say?"

"She hit me on the face with her hand," he repeated as he felt tentatively of his unmarked cheek. He was perhaps the youngest of the men and had not been much noticed before.

"What did you do?"

"You fool! What did you do?"

"He sure did something! Speak up, Skyboy! What did you do?"

"Nothing! I only walked up to her! I didn't know! I wanted to ask if I should move the horses before night."

"Listen! We won't stand for this! You did something!"

Elk Head pushed through them and confronted the young man. "All right, what happened? Stop lying! Tell the truth!"

"It's the truth! I didn't know she was up there crying."

"What?"

"What did he say?"

"You fool! We won't stand for this! We'll cut out your lying, forked tongue!"

"It's the truth! I walked up to her and I thought something was the matter and I said, 'What's the matter?' And when she looked up she was crying, and when she saw me look at her, she struck me. That's all that happened."

"Are you crazy?" Elk Head asked. "She was not crying! You must be out of your mind to say that!"

"That fool! He did something!"

"We won't stand for it!"

"Make him tell what happened!"

Elk Head insisted, "She was not crying!"

"I thought she was."

"Why would she be crying, you idiot! You are in trouble, young man. This is serious! If Woman Chief has any complaint against you, then we certainly won't have any mercy on you!"

The young man was troubled and would only say, "I thought she was." He backed away from the fire and from the others, to stand with great uncertainty. All of them looked at him with disgust.

When Woman Chief returned, they saw nothing unusual about her, and she did not seem to notice any trouble in the camp. She gave some brief orders about a guard and putting out the fire and she wanted to move on south before daybreak; then she rolled up in a robe a short distance away. The men began to prepare for a night's sleep, though the sun had barely sunk below the jagged hills.

Skyboy seemed to have realized finally what a montrous thing he had done or said. If what he had said were a lie, he deserved any punishment they might exact, and if it were true, they could never forgive him for knowing about it and saying it. He spoke only briefly and in a low voice to one other warrior. "Tell Sweet Thunder Woman I am sorry. I am going home now." Then he walked off in the dusk, going southeast, carrying his rifle, but seemingly having forgotten about his two horses.

They would never see him again. Some of them might have stopped him without much trouble. He was not going in exactly the right direction and was in enemy country alone in treacherous weather. Perhaps they felt that his departure was the only solution. They had seen much war and death in recent weeks and could not afford to think certain thoughts about their leader. Their feelings about

her were stronger than they had felt about any other leader, but they were also ambiguous. Those
who knew that she had wept at the death of Ride
Away had now put the memory out of their minds
and would have denied it if reminded.

When they came down to Big River, or as some
said Big Muddy, it was solid ice. Scouting down it,
they located five Atsina hunters in a point of
timber, ambushed and killed them, and took their
packs of elk meat. Three of the twenty-seven Crow
warriors were wounded, two so seriously that they
could barely ride.

They pushed south between the mountains and
over the rolling hills toward the Musselshell. Winter cme on them in all its violence. Snow as dry as
powder blew level in the wind, sometimes so thick
that the party had difficulty keeping together. It
built up knee-deep to the horses on level ground
and deeper than a horse is tall in drifts along the
coulees. There was no point in scouting; any enemy
in the country was fighting the weather.

For six days they struggled desperately against
the blizzard. It was hard to find firewood and hard
to start a fire even with the use of gunpowder.
Among their booty they had two pack loads of
shelled corn, which they fed to their horses; still the
horses suffered greatly and began dropping dead of
the cold. The men slept under the lee of banks,
bundling together and allowing the blowing snow
to cover them. Woman Chief slept under a single
robe with the two badly wounded, one of whom
had been shot in the leg and neck, the other in the
chest.

In these troubles, the men followed her with as

much loyalty and confidence as they had followed her in fighting. They believed that she understood winter and knew how to survive and what direction to go in those fierce days when the sky was darker than the land.

When finally she brought them across Elk River and to High Owl's winter camp on Thick Ash Tree Creek, a third of their horses were gone. Twenty-six of the original thirty men remained alive. Several of the party had lost fingers or toes from frostbite. But, besides some modest booty of trade goods, they brought twenty-nine enemy scalps. Those who feared the eventual extermination of the Crows by surrounding enemies now believed that the danger from the north had decreased.

By the time new grass began to start in the spring, warriors from other Crow bands were asking to join her. She led a hundred men east against the Sioux in a fast slashing foray that left a trail of blood from the mouth of Elk River south to the Black Hills. Upon her return she rested and took part in a communal buffalo hunt. Then in early summer she struck southeast, leading two hundred and fifty fighting men. On this expedition the Crows caught a Cheyenne band strung out in the process of moving camp, killed half of the enemy warriors, took all the property they could carry, and scattered the survivors like scared prairie chickens.

Returning from this raid, Woman Chief and those from High Owl's band found that the old chief had died a natural death. The council has procrastinated about naming a successor until her return. They met now expecting a long, difficult, delicate discussion, for Rainy was the senior mem-

ber among those who had taken a leadership role.
And could a woman be a civil chief? Even if she
was the most brilliant war leader in the tribe? Did
she want it?

She made the man civil chief of the band with a
mere nod of her head. There was no problem, delicate or otherwise. Hereafter it would be known as
Rainy's band. The council members realized with a
small start of surprise how wise she always was,
how little it mattered whose band it was said to be.

Woman Chief had killed a cow elk at a water
hole early in the morning, and Bad Woman had
come to help butcher it. They cut the hide down the
backbone, and while they were turning the carcass
back and forth on the grass to skin it, Bad Woman
said: "You shouldn't be doing this work. A chief
has more important things to do."

"The most important thing right now is to do
something with this meat," Woman Chief said.
"We'll have to give most of it away. It should all be
cooking or smoking or drying by this time tomorrow, or it will spoil."

"But you could tell Birdy to help me. It's not
right for a chief to do this kind of work."

"Oh, shut up talking like a slave! Let's put all the
pieces to slice thin and dry on one hide half and the
rest on the other."

They worked in silence awhile, only mentioning
who might be given the liver, the heart, a slab of
ribs. Then Woman Chief asked, "Have you
thought about what I asked you to do one time?
About having a baby?"

Bad Woman did not answer at once, but finally
said, "It was only a kind of joke. I couldn't do anything like that."

"No, it wasn't a joke. Not to me, it wasn't. You could do it if you wanted to."

"How could I do it? Look at me! I couldn't do anything like that at all."

Woman Chief insisted, "You could if you wanted to! You have a good figure. You could flirt with a man. I told you about Little Wolf, who is partly blind, and there are plenty of men. You are wasting your life! You could have a baby for our lodge!"

The woman hacked at a stubborn joint with her heavy knife, then looked at Woman Chief as if to see whether she was as serious, even angry, as she sounded. "You don't understand! I just couldn't do it."

"I don't see why not! You said that I saved your life once! Now, you say I'm a chief! Why can't you do something to please me? Why do you want to be so stubborn?"

"I earn my place in the lodge by hard work."

"But you are wasting your life! Can't you see that? Why are you so stubborn?"

"You don't understand."

"You don't understand me either," Woman Chief said.

They completed the work in silence and did not speak as they loaded the pack horse and carried the meat into camp. Perhaps each waited for the other to say some kind word. After she had distributed some of the meat, Woman Chief caught Little Smoke and rode out to move the horse herd of the lodge to some better pasture.

When she returned in the middle of the afternoon, Birdy, alone at the lodge and greatly agitated, informed her that Bad Woman had run away. "I begged her and begged her, but she wouldn't listen," Birdy said. "She just put her things in a bundle and ran away."

Antelope Man was off gambling with some other men. See Dead Bull had come in after the departure of Bad Woman and had finally decided to pursue the woman and try to bring her back. Birdy, nearly crying, said, "She didn't steal anything. She wouldn't even take the jewelry and blankets you gave her. She only took her clothes and a little dried meat."

"Why did she say she was leaving?"

"She wouldn't tell me. I begged her and begged her."

"Which way did she go?"

"Up that way." Birdy pointed west. The land was a series of ridges and swells.

Woman Chief rode out of camp to the rising ground in the west. When she could see some distance ahead, she pulled up and studied the terrain to try to guess what route Bad Woman had taken. Farther on in a low area she found the tracks of the two women, those of See Dead Bull slightly heavier than the ones she followed. So Woman Chief progressed, riding fast from one place to the next where tracks might be preserved.

She caught up with her foster mother in an hour. See Dead Bull was concerned that she had lost the trail, but in the next low ground they found the tracks again. Woman Chief was walking and leading Little Smoke. The older woman panted and sweated from the fast walking, but would not ride the horse. She said, "I'm afraid we won't catch her. At least I want to apologize. I wish I hadn't scolded her."

"Why did you scold her?"

"She had let the fire go out. I don't know why I was so mean."

"I scolded her too," Woman Chief said.

"Why did you scold her?"

They walked side by side, and Woman Chief waited a long while before she answered. "I don't know why. For no reason. I told her something and we didn't agree, so I got mad at her. She wouldn't do what I asked. I don't know why I got mad. She's cut up that way—her nose looks bad, and she has to face the world every day saying she was not a faithful woman, so I guess I thought I could treat her any way and it didn't matter."

"What did you ask her to do?"

"I wanted her to flirt with a man who is nearly blind and have a baby for our lodge. It's foolish. It's crazy. Why did I treat her that way?"

As she plodded along, See Dead Bull began to sniff and wipe her eyes. She said, "Every person has a trouble or many troubles. It's hard to be kind to each other. I always want a respectable lodge, but I haven't treated other people right." She stumbled on a tuft of grass and her voice broke as she went on. "We have to find her! I have to apologize. Oh, Horse Tender!"

It meant something more than she had said, something about her own baby boy dead in the river, and about a little captive girl who was beaten by her foster mother. Woman Chief patted her on the shoulder briefly as they walked. It was the first friendly touching between them.

When they first saw Bad Woman ahead, she had already seen them and had begun to run, but she soon stopped, squatted down in the grass, and pulled her blanket tight over her head. She would not look at See Dead Bull and Woman Chief.

Though each of them apologized and asked her to return home, she made no sound, but to the question as to where she was going, she replied, "Nowhere."

"Are you going to live here, sitting in the grass?" See Dead Bull asked.

No answer.

"You'll have to come home," Woman Chief said. "We can't do without you. We need you."

No answer.

See Dead Bull asserted, "We're going to capture you and make a slave out of you. Then you'll have to obey and come home."

"Let's get some sticks and start beating her," Woman Chief suggested.

Bad Woman would not respond.

After a while they began to talk about her almost as if she were not there, or could not hear. About why she must have felt she had to leave and how it must feel to be mutilated in a way that was a clear sign or message to all who saw her. The shame was not that she had done wrong, for most men and many women had done the same, but that she had to admit it every time a person looked at her. Men are cruel. See Dead Bull began once more to bemoan the fact that people are thoughtless and do not treat each other kindly, until finally she began to weep, as did Woman Chief.

Bad Woman lowered her covering blanket and said, "Well, it's no wonder men look down on women, the way they stand around on the prairie blubbering."

Woman Chief said, "It looks to me like you're crying too, you old fraud!"

The three of them began laughing with their tears. Bad Woman stood up, and the other two came and hugged her.

See Dead Bull, still sniffing, asked, "Did you ever see such a worthless slave, Horse Tender? We have to worry about her and waste time chasing her, so she won't run off and get lost."

"Yes, and she won't obey our orders or even pay attention to us."

"What do you think we should do to her?"

"Something terrible," Woman Chief said. "We'll think of something. Now we'd better start back. It will be dark before we get home."

Bad Woman said, "You don't really need me in the lodge."

"Yes, we do," See Dead Bull said quickly.

"You are going back with us," Woman Chief said. "If you don't, we'll just stay out here with you on the prairie. We won't go back if you don't. Come on, I'll help you on the horse." Little Smoke was nibbling at the grass and watching them as if he understood their conversation.

"I don't want to ride that war-horse!"

"Go ahead," See Dead Bull told her. "You have to obey Horse Tender. She's a chief."

"Let her boss the men. I'll walk."

Woman Chief said, "Well, you have to obey See Dead Bull. She's the first woman of the lodge."

"Let her boss Antelope Man and Birdy."

They laughed some more and started home, leading the war-horse. Their tears and laughter, pleadings and embarrassment and teasing, had made them friends as they had never been before.

15. The Great Conference

Rumors had begun to travel over Crow country, carried by traders and those visiting other bands. The white people away in the east wanted to have a great meeting of Plains Indian people. It was all rather vague and mysterious. They had heard traders and white soldiers speak of a Great White Father, who seemed to presume that even Crows were subject to him in some way. What his fighting strength might be nobody knew, but he was an excellent trading partner, for he had iron in his land and his people knew how to make things out of iron, as well as gunpowder and fine cloth and beads. There was some kind of white person called an *agent,* who wanted the great meeting.

The council of Rainy's band talked about it, but did not have enough information. They needed to make at least a tentative decision before the approaching Tobacco Planting gathering of the tribe, for it would be a tribal involvement if any Crows took part. Finally, Rainy brought Chicago to the council circle to tell them what he could. The old trader evidently felt at ease smoking and talking with the leaders of the band. He began, as did many an Indian orator, by stating his general point of view.

"You know me," he said. "I ain't no stranger. I'm Crow. A long time ago I was a white man. I ain't anymore. I trade with people all over, but I don't trade with the damn Sioux and Blackfeet, ner any of our enemies. If we get in a war with the whites or anybody else, I'll fight on the side of the Crows. You know me. And I don't lie to you.

"The main thing I got to say is this: the white agent is called Broken Hand Fitzpatrick. You can trust him. I know him. I've known Broken Hand nigh onto thirty years and I say you can trust him. That's the main thing I got to say."

When he paused, Woman Chief said, "Can our enemies trust him too?"

Chicago scratched his head a minute. "I reckon they can."

"Can he trust them?"

"Well, now . . . look," Chicago said, "I ain't here to take sides, but to say what I know. That's all."

She persisted. "Does he know the difference between friends and enemies?"

"He knows the Crow don't kill no white people, and the Shonshonis don't."

Rainy asked, "What do you think this Broken Hand wants?"

"Well, from what I hear he wants all the Indians and the whites to have a big council some place down on the Platte this coming fall."

"To do what?"

"Make peace. All I can do is guess, but I would say the whites want to cut out the raiding and fighting. All of it. They might try to decide on lines where the Crows can live and hunt. Then I guess they want roads across the country and would give presents and goods for payment. I ain't taking no sides, but I judge we got more enemies than friends, and it wouldn't hurt to listen to the whites."

Woman Chief asked, "Is Broken Hand your friend?"

"He used to be. Now I got no friends except Crow people."

They discussed the matter around the circle, tentatively, most of them saying little or repeating what had already been said. They were searching for a basis for consensus so that Rainy's band could approach the Crow Nation with one mind.

Finally Woman Chief said, "I'm against it. I understand that the Great White Father intends to enforce a peace. If he had ten thousand soldiers, he could do it. He could control our enemies, and I would gladly accept peace. But does he have that many soldiers? Or does he expect us to risk everything we have by trusting people we cannot afford to trust?"

After a moment of silence, Chicago said, "Reckon the Blackfeet and Lakota and Cheyenne are holding council right now and wondering can they trust us? They've got the worst of it the last few years. Maybe they would gladly accept peace."

She answered him quickly. "Yes, they would gladly take our homeland. Who is the aggressor? Do we try to push them back and take their land? Listen, Crow chiefs! To live is to fight! We can do no less for our children. The Earth is a land of conflict. Our lives tell us it is so. We can defend ourselves or surrender to those who hate us. I have no more to say on the subject."

* * *

As they moved toward the grounds for the Tobacco Planting gathering, the leaders of Rainy's band were troubled, for the news from other bands seemed to indicate that most Crows favored attending the approaching peace conference. Yet none of the tribe could go if one band refused. It seemed that Rainy's band was going to refuse.

The Crow Nation in the ancient past had grown corn, squash, pumpkins, and other crops. They still had a covenant with the Earth, that they might fertilize the soil by burning brush and grass, then plant the sacred tobacco seed and return later to gather the crop. The planting was a reminder to the Earth of the covenant and a reassurance to themselves. They gathered this year on Arrow Creek, at a place where the grass grew lush and the timber was open.

Antelope Man's two tepees had been set up, but there was still unpacking and arranging to do. Antelope Man had been hiring the services of a young warrior to help with the horse tending, and Woman Chief showed the young man where to pasture the stock. When she returned to the newly set up lodge, Chicago had come looking for her.

"Little Gal," he said, "I want you to go on a short visit with me."

"Visiting? I thought maybe you were mad at me."

"I don't get mad at nobody, Little Gal. Getting too old. It upsets my stomach to get mad."

"Visit? Where?"

"Just right down yonder."

"What for? You can talk to me here."

"I want to show you a couple of things, Little

Gal. Don't keep on asking me questions. Just come on."

They walked down among the lodges of the gathering bands. The people were busy, but some of them stared at Woman Chief and some greeted Chicago. He would grunt in response as he hobbled along. They approached a small tepee away from the others; the leather covering of the dwelling had been patched in several places. Chicago stopped and she stopped.

They watched two small children playing about the trunk of a cottonwood tree beside the ragged tepee. The little girl was something over two winters in age, the little boy something over three, both naked. One would toddle around behind the tree and pretend to hide, then they would peek around and discover each other. They squealed and laughed and seemed to take endless delight in the innocent game. When the chubby girl fell on account of her excess exuberance, the boy clumsily helped her to her feet, and they went back to their play.

Woman Chief was entranced. Finally she said, "You were going to show me a couple of things."

"Yes."

"What is this, Chicago? Is this where we are going to visit?"

He said, "Don't they put you in mind of a couple of pups playing?"

"No, they don't. They are the most beautiful children I have ever seen."

He was rummaging in a big coat pocket. "Little Gal, I found this here candy in the bottom of a bag of junk. No telling how long they had been rolling around in there, but it don't look dirty or ruined."

He handed her two pieces of hard yellow candy, each half as big as his thumb.

"What's this for? Look, Chicago, I don't know what you think you're doing. We disagree about the peace conference this fall, even though you said you don't take sides. What is it? Do you imagine that you will show me two darling Crow babies and I will change my mind and start loving my enemies? Are you going to soften my hard heart? You know how much I would like to give them these sweets, and you take advantage of me. I not only think you're stupid, I don't even think it's fair."

"Little Gal . . ."

"You can stop calling me pet names. I don't think it's fair."

"Well, you asked for my help one time. I tried to help you, but you wouldn't listen. I'm trying again. Did you ever pray for a baby? Reckon you would know if your prayer was answered?"

"Chicago, what right do you have to meddle this way? You think you're so wise. I don't want an old man meddling around with me this way." She was gripping the pieces of candy. When she opened her hand, it was sweaty, and the candy was becoming sticky. "What do you mean . . . if my prayer was answered?"

"Their mother and father is both dead, Little Gal. This here lodge belongs to their grandmother's sister. And she knows she can't keep the kids. Why don't you give them the candy?"

"It's dirty."

He strode forward and picked up a stomach bag of water near the tepee door, came back, and sloshed it over her hand. Then, standing by the closed flap, he spoke in a loud voice. "Old lady! Come out here! We want to talk to you! Come out here!"

Woman Chief approached the children and found that they were not afraid.

An old woman came out of the tepee, and Chicago asked, "What did you ever decide to do with the babies?"

She sounded a little like Pea Finder. "I don't know. I could go live with my son-in-law, but I can't take the babies."

"Would you give them to a lodge in Rainy's band?"

"I would. If they would take good care of them."

Woman Chief had the two children squatting on the ground with the candy in their mouths. She was saying to them, "Now, don't bite it. It will hurt your teeth. Is it good?" They nodded with great solemnity and busily moved the strange new food around in their mouths.

She would not let Chicago help carry them, but carried one on each arm. And she would not let him go back to ask the old woman their names, for she said she had known their names for a long time. The boy was Brave Rider and the girl was Pink Morning.

During two days while the Crows were gathering and setting up their camps Woman Chief played with the children. She took them to a beach on the creek where the water ran ankle-deep over clean sand and gravel, and sat down to watch them splash and laugh and dig sand. Soon Antelope Man came to watch, then Bad Woman, finally Birdy and See Dead Bull.

They stuffed the children with every kind of food and watched over them while they slept, until finally Antelope Man said, "All you women should get to work. Woman Chief and I can take care of my grandchildren by ourself."

They did not pay too much attention to him. On the afternoon of the second day, he proposed, "We have to try to locate two gentle ponies we can trade for. Someone can lead the ponies, and I can walk alongside to hold the children on them."

That evening Woman Chief went to Rainy's lodge and asked him, "Does the all-Crow council meet tomorrow?"

"Yes, in the afternoon."

"I want to speak to Rainy's council in the morning."

"What time?"

"Very soon after sunup."

The chief agreed.

There was no other business for the council that morning except the words of Woman Chief. "This afternoon," she said to them, "you will send three or four of us to speak and listen at the all-Crow council. Our fellow chiefs will want to know where we stand on the white man peace conference.

"I believe we must keep an open mind. We know we can trust Chicago. He says we can trust the agent Broken Hand. We should be suspicious of our enemies and guard against treachery, but enemies can never make peace unless there is a little trust to start with. Without trust, war would go on forever.

"We have punished the evil tribes who crowd us, and they have punished us. The question is, Would they be willing to stop? It is better to get horses by

breeding than by stealing. It is better to get food
and goods by hunting and gathering and trading
than by stealing. Perhaps our enemies are beginning to realize that they cannot take our land without great losses to themselves.

"Then it may be that we should try to please the
white people. If their peace fails, we would do well
to have them for allies. My advice is that we keep
an open mind, but always protect ourselves and
watch out for treachery."

They agreed with her and no one remarked on
the fact that she had advised the opposite a few
days before.

During that summer the Crow Nation moved
southeast in several groups, continuously scouting
and maintaining communication among themselves. Several chiefs went with a party of whites
and Assinboin and Minnetarees, headed by a white
trader and a white medicine man named DeSmet.
That party foolishly took wagons over the rugged
terrain and would arrive late at the treaty grounds.
The other group of Crows hunted as they moved
southeast and frequently sent runners from one
camp to another. When they saw other Indians,
they detoured around them.

In the hottest days of late summer, the Crows
crossed the barren headwaters of the Powder and
camped along a creek running south toward what
is called the North Platte. At this camp they would
keep the main body of the warriors for the protection of the people. A delegation, including Rainy,
Woman Chief, Chicago, and chiefs from every
Crow band, went on south with some wives and
horse tenders and runners, taking tepees and food

supplies. They passed a trading post called Fort Laramie and moved on downriver to a huge encampment on Horse Creek.

Some nine tribes or their representatives had gathered, in all as many as ten thousand Indians. Their lodges spread out in every direction. Canvas-covered tents for the white soldiers were lined in neat rows. The Crow delegation pitched their tepees near those of the Shoshonis. Horses dotted the plains in every direction as far as the eye could reach. No one could keep from being impressed with the sight of smoke curling up from a thousand fires and the many strange people passing to and fro.

Woman Chief and Chicago had a lodge in common with Rainy and two of his wives. They had scarcely gotten settled when Chicago hobbled off to hunt up two white friends, the Broken Hand he had spoken of and another named Bridger. The two men obviously were eager to see and talk to Woman Chief. And they were not the only ones interested, for children and people of all ages were approaching the Crow camp to catch sight of her, stare a moment, then go back.

The strange white men had brought coffee, which one of Rainy's wives hastened to boil and serve. The conversation was a mixture of speech and sign language, with the strange white men speaking mostly English and Woman Chief and Rainy speaking mostly Crow, with Chicago trying to interpret. They assured the Crows that the encampment seemed safe; already enemy tribes had been exchanging visits. Then the talk turned to possible peace treaties; Woman Chief said that she was mainly concerned with a guarantee of boundaries and the exact location of the lines.

Bridger was talking about the possible limits of the Crow homeland, and Chicago was trying to interpret.

Woman Chief interrupted. "He did not say the Musselshell River, Chicago. He said the valley of the Musselshell."

Bridger asked, "Does she speak English?"

"Law," Chicago said, "I don't know. She speaks three or four Indian languages."

"Do you speak English?"

"No," she said.

"No," Chicago repeated in English.

"Then how do you understand what I ask?"

"Because I know a few words and I guess what you have in mind."

Chicago repeated, "Because she knows a few words and guesses what you got in mind."

The agent Broken Hand and Bridger looked at each other in amazement and laughed.

"But let's get back to the Musselshell," she said. "If land goes *to* the valley, that is one thing. If the land goes to the stream, that's another. If the land *includes* the valley, that's still another. I hope that if the whites intend to make a peace and enforce it, they will be exact in language."

"Yes," Rainy said. "They should say exactly what they mean."

Both of the whites assured them that there would be careful interpretation of everything. There were both whites and Indians who spoke two languages. Broken Hand asked Woman Chief if she wanted to be an interpreter.

"No," she said, "but I want to hear what you say when you tell other tribes the bounds of Crow land."

He laughed. "No matter what the language, you

will know a few words and guess what the inter-
preters say?"

Without waiting for Chicago to put his words
into Crow, she said, "That's right."

The conference amounted to an endless suc-
cession of speeches. The white officials sat at a long
table in front of their big tents, and a broad half
circle of chairs had been provided for the chiefs,
though most of them preferred to sit on the
ground. Behind them stretched many Indians, sitting or standing or wandering around. When anyone spoke, he had to pause frequently; then would
come a babble as the words were put into all the
languages. In some cases, an interpreter had to listen to another interpreter before he could put the
ideas into the tongue he was supposed to. Many
speakers were pompous and boring. There was
more excitement in so many tribes being together
than in what was said.

The Crows found that Chicago had told them
accurately the general intentions of the whites.
Strange Indians often wandered by the delegation
to look at Woman Chief. Also, those seated frequently stared at her.

They found that the negotiation and specif-
ication of tribal boundaries would not be taken up
for five days. Since Rainy wanted to send a messen-
ger back to the main Crow camp to tell them all
was well, Woman Chief said she would go. Chicago, teasing her, said she wanted to get away from
all the strangers staring at her.

Rainy asked, "You'll be sure to come back?"

"Yes, I'll come back."

She rode through the long night and the next

morning to the Crow camp and was pleased to see wolves out guarding it. As she passed the tepees strung out along the creek, she told the people that all was well at the peace conference. At the lodge of Antelope Man, the children Brave Rider and Pink Morning were taking a nap, and she lay down on the robe with them to sleep.

For three days she stayed with the familiar people of her own band and her own tribe, spending much time playing with the two children in the creek water or holding them while they slept. Then she made the long ride back to the treaty grounds, taking with her two men and their wives who wanted to go.

The strangers still stared at her wherever she went. Chicago by this time resented the stares; he said that half the men in the vast gathering were afraid of her.

When the conference took up the issue of tribal boundaries, Woman Chief worked through Rainy, and he worked with and through other Crow chiefs. Three problems seemed to be of concern to her: that all should understand the meaning of a nation's lines, that no foreign people could hunt there without permission; that the boundaries should be set exactly; and that the interpretations into the languages should be clear, so that every people understood the same as others understood.

For an entire half day Woman Chief dominated the conference, whites and all, with her continual insistence that the real problems be addressed clearly, not in pompous rhetoric. When finally near sundown the Crow lines were set and explained to her satisfaction, the leading white commissioner mopped his forehead with a white cloth and said,

"We hope that the Crow Nation is now satisfied."
The Crow chiefs whispered to Rainy, who exchanged whispers with Woman Chief, then went
back and whispered with his colleagues; one of
them rose and announced to the white commis-
sioners and all others: "The Crow Nation is now
satisfied."

They had got boundaries they could live with,
thus: In the direction of the Star that Does Not
Move, the channel of the Musselshell. In the direction of the sunrise, the channel of the Powder. In
the direction of Summer, or away from the Star
that Does Not Move, the channels of Wind River
and Rattlesnake Creek. In the direction of sunset,
the highest waters of Elk River.

The whites had promised presents of trade goods
that would be brought in a few days by a wagon
train, and the Indians waited on the treaty
grounds. They spent the time dancing and visiting.
Many came out of curiosity into the Crow camp
just to see Woman Chief. Three strange women
brought a freshly dressed antelope to give her, and
they had brought their children; obviously they
wanted their children to be able to say they had
seen Woman Chief. The most unusual of these visits was that of two *berdaches* dressed like women,
whose tribe could not be identified; they were not
Crow. They timidly presented to Woman Chief a
soft-tanned doeskin worked with an elaborate pattern of beadwork. Rumor even said that the enemy
peoples were singing parts of songs about her;
perhaps they had picked them up earlier through
the Hidatsa or Shoshone.

But the greatest reaction to her seemed to be
fear, as Chicago had said. If she walked with one of

Rainy's wives over to the stream to carry water, children scurried into tepees, conversations stopped, and heads turned to stare. It was easy to guess that many a silent enemy thought: It would be easy to kill her now; one arrow or one bullet would do it.

Woman Chief decided not to wait for the whites' wagon train, but made the long ride back to the all-Crow camp alone. The other chiefs followed in two days. Then the Crows trecked back northwest into the homeland that had been guaranteed to them, there to make winter camps band by band. The white man would prove unable to buy or impose his peace at so early a date, but the Crow Nation had won an easing of the pressure on themselves for a time, and recognition of their right to exist.

16. The Last Battle

She came before the tepee of Chicago, cleared her throat, stood a minute, finally called his name in a conversational tone, then in a loud voice. His wife stuck her head out, uttered a little sound of recognition, and ducked back in. Woman Chief waited. It was a good day of early summer, with lumpy clouds floating in the sky. After some rustling and grunting, Chicago emerged clumsily.

He had aged considerably during the past year or so. His hair and unruly beard were as white as the top of a mountain. His back was humped and his limbs did not obey him well, but his eyes seemed as alive as ever. He grouched, "Some of these big chiefs think they can wake a man up any hour of the day or night."

She laughed. "What a trader you are! Big deals in the wind and you're asleep."

"Big deals!" he said. "If I trade off my stuff, then I won't have anything to trade." He scratched himself here and there; he seemed uncomfortable.

Suddenly he said to her, "Little Gal, please don't go! You don't have to! Please don't go!"

"Why, Chicago, it's already decided."

"By who?"

"By Rainy's council."

"The council don't decide nothing unless you tell them to. I say you don't have to go!"

"Look, the Crows have exchanged visits with all our old enemies except the Atsinas. I think it's important that we make a gesture of trust and friendship."

"But why you?"

She laughed. "I'm the only one who speaks Atsina."

"That ain't the whole of it. Let them visit here. You don't have to go. You're trusting people too far."

"Why, Chicago, our men and women and even children have been welcomed in enemy camps. And given presents."

"And ain't one of them got the war record you got. Them savages have got a reason for revenge against you. Quit trying to fool an old trader like me, Little Gal. I know a dozen men wanted to go with you. I know what goes on. I know the five you picked to go. Not one of them is the only hunter in his family. Not one of the five but could be spared if he was murdered. And you done it on purpose. You picked them. I'm asking you please don't go, Little Gal."

She had become solemn. "I have to go and try. It's a special feeling."

"You ain't no Atsina," he said quickly. "You don't owe them a thing."

"No, that's true, Chicago. But I have this special feeling. I have to go to them."

"Women!" he said. "How come they always got some mysterious feelings to where they got to do something that don't make sense?"

"Look, don't worry. It's just a feeling. It may be the last trip I'll ever make out of Crow country, now that raiding is over. Maybe I'll even stop being a warrior. Anyway, it seems like I'm bound, you know, or called to go." She suddenly laughed. "Oh, Chicago, how could I expect you to understand? What I came to tell you is this: You can have the Spanish saddle with the silver on it. Consider it a gift from me. But I want you to be on the lookout for the ponies for Brave Rider and Pink Morning. I'll pay whatever they cost you. Will you do it?"

"I reckon so."

"Chicago, you're the best friend a girl ever had."

"Little Gal, if you'll give up this nonsense about going to visit the Atsinas, I'll get you the pet horses for your babies and it won't cost you a cent."

"It's already decided, Chicago."

Apparently he accepted the hopelessness of his position, for he threw up his gnarled hands and began grumbling words that could not be understood.

Back at the lodge of Antelope Man, she put together the small packs of food she would need on the journey. They would leave in the morning. Birdy said to her, "Why are you giving so many presents, even to Chicago? You have given me and See Dead Bull and Bad Woman jewelry and other presents. You have given away your best things."

"I just feel good toward everyone, Birdy."

"But you have given away all your prettiest things."

See Dead Bull brought a tiny doll dress that she was beading to show them. The women were making dolls, a small horn bow, and other toys for the two children, now just the age to jabber and be petted. Antelope Man's first wife had never called Woman Chief daughter, but she now tried to please all the persons in the lodge and had already said that she would teach Pink Morning to be a tepee cutter.

Legend would embellish Woman Chief's attempt to visit the Atsinas. As it would make her more beautiful, more wise, more generous, than she deserved from her real life, so it would suggest a supernatural medicine moving her in these days. A song years ago had asked: "What has Man Alone sent to the Crow Nation?" Legend would imply that in some certain fullness of time she was called back to where she came from.

They rode north at a slow pace, for Woman Chief had brought no other horse besides Little Smoke, who had lost his youthful stamina, though he was still a handsome mount. The five men had followed her in war, and they deferred to her and obeyed her now. They sent out no wolves and posted no guards. The procession was somewhat formal.

The land where the Atsina lived was vivid green under the early summer sun, as only grass and leaves can be when they have waited long under a hard winter. The trees and brush along the watercourses were full of busy nesting birds. Woman Chief and the five warriors entered a wide belt of timber in a valley and came into an opening that would have made a beautiful campsite for an Indian band.

They surprised a party of strangers, some dozen men, who may have been out hunting. Their horses were staked around the edge of the clearing.

"We want to be friends," Woman Chief called in Atsina. "We come to visit."

The strangers were scrambling for their weapons and toward their tied horses.

"We want to be friends," she called again, continuing to move toward them. When she had ridden as close as twenty steps from the nearest, and the strangers surrounded her on three sides, she said to the five Crow men, "Drop your weapons on the ground." They obeyed.

Whether it was from fear or revenge or some motive they did not understand, the Atsinas opened fire. One Crow yelled, "Run!" even as an arrow struck his throat. They no more than wheeled their horses before they were all hit. It was over as quickly as it took a dozen men to each fire one musket ball and two or three arrows. Then the Atsinas fled from the scene, leaving behind them no movement other than the kicking of horses sprawled in the lush grass.

Rumors and true news have a way of traveling distances well-nigh magically. It must be that they are carried by riders or runners, yet no one can say exactly how. From the glade where the six Crow bodies lay, information went out in the four directions to the various people: Nez Perce, Flathead, Piegan, Assinboin, Atsina, Mandan, Arikara, Minnetaree, Lakota, Cheyenne, Pawnee, Shoshone.

More than her own tribe mourned her. The allies. Recent friends. Even among enemies some who were romantic or superstitious or frustrated. Somewhere a Blackfoot woman scratched her breast with the point of a butcher knife and

moaned her grief for a sister woman; strong
Cheyenne men shook their heads and remained silent, looking past their companions to whatever
the distance means. A Shoshone singer, trying to
repeat the Crow words of a song about her, choked
up.

If news travels fast by an unknown route,
perhaps the turned-loose spirit of a person goes
even more swiftly and mysteriously. Antelope Man
lay on a robe in the dooryard, and the women and
two children bent over him frequently and watched
him, for he had been unable to take food for three
days. Suddenly, his face became animated.

"Father, are you awake?"

He smiled at her. It was a joke between them.

"Father, are you asleep?"

"You cannot tease me, Horse Tender, and worry
me like you once did. How strong and beautiful
you have become. You are like all good daughters
and all strong songs put together! I used to be
afraid someone would hurt you; I had forgotten
how you knocked down a Crow warrior with a
quarter of deer that was big as you were at the
time.

"What did you say? Yes, everything will be all
right. I think so. I'm going to give you a new name
I heard the *berdaches* and the camp children say."

Bad Woman brought a horn of water and knelt
waiting beside the others, holding one hand over
her nose. Birdy said, "He's whispering something."

See Dead Bull said, "He's talking to our daughter and calling her Sweet Thunder Woman. He has
lost his mind."

But his old, worn face looked for a minute as if
he were enjoying a small joke with a friend.

Benjamin Capps was born in Dundee, Texas in 1922. He grew up on the land, the son of a working cowboy who rode horseback to a one-room schoolhouse for his elementary education. He attended Texas Technological College in 1939. During the Second World War he was in the U.S. Army Air Corps and served in the Pacific theater. After discharge, Capps returned to pursue higher education, obtaining a bachelor's degree in 1948 and a masters degree in 1949 from the University of Texas. For the next few years he taught English and journalism at Northeastern State College in Tahlequah, Oklahoma, before changing his course in life entirely, entering industry as a tool-and-die maker, at which trade he worked for the next decade while he wrote Western fiction.

Capps' first published literary effort was *Hanging at Comanche Wells* (1962), a paperback original that was never reprinted until it was published in a new hardcover edition by Chivers Press, Ltd., in 2001. *The Trail to Ogallala* (1964) followed, the story of a cattle drive from Texas to Nebraska. This novel won a Spur Award from the Western Writers of America, as did Capps' next novel, *Sam Chance* (1965) as well as his much later short story collection, *Tales of the Southwest* (1991). Virtually all of Capps' Western novels and stories depict with ambivalence the struggle for survival on the Western frontier. Later novels tend to focus unforgettably on the lives of American Indians, such as A *Woman of the People* (1966) and *The White Man's Road* (1969), the latter an unusually grim, albeit wholly realistic, view of reservation life among the Comanches. Capps' Western stories display such uniform mastery that they cannot so much be analyzed as they must be experienced. One of the author's recurring themes is how the American Indian tended to live by visions whereas the Anglo-American most often lived by dreams, and how in various, sometimes bitterly painful ways, these visions and dreams would clash with physical and social reality. *Mesquite Country* is Benjamin Capps' most recent novel.